The M
For Bringing Out The Worst in Her,

Anne Richmond thought.

Then why, heaven help her, was she so aware of him? Why did she keep noticing such disturbing things about him—the film of perspiration in the hollow of his tanned, strongly corded neck, the way his powerful thigh muscles rippled sensuously in his snug jeans?

This man shouldn't be sexy, she thought in a panic. By every definition of what she had always considered appealing in a male, Ross McIntyre had no right to his sexiness. There was too much of him—too much solid height, too many sharp angles on his lean face, too much force in his gruff voice. Too much of everything but the sensitivity she prized in a man. Then why couldn't she control her awareness of him?

And how was she supposed to stand the upriver haul in his close company?

Dear Reader:

Happy New Year! 1991 is going to be a terrific year at Silhouette Desire. We've got some wonderful things planned, starting with another of those enticing, irresistible, tantalizing men. Yes, *Man of the Month* will continue through 1991!

Man of the Month kicks off with *Nelson's Brand* by Diana Palmer. If you remember, Diana Palmer launched *Man of the Month* in 1989 with her fabulous book, *Reluctant Father*. I'm happy to say that *Nelson's Brand* is another winner—it's sensuous, highly charged and the hero, Gene Nelson, is a man you'll never forget.

But January is not only *Man of the Month*. This month, look out for additional love stories, starting with the delightful *Four Dollars and Fifty-One Cents* by Lass Small. And no, I'm not going to tell you what the title means—you'll have to read the book! There's also another great story by Carole Buck, *Paradise Remembered,* a sexy adventure by Jean Barrett, *Heat,* and a real charmer from Cathie Linz, *Handyman*. You'll also notice a new name, Ryanne Corey. But I'm sure you'll want to know that she's already written a number of fine romances as Courtney Ryan. Believe me, *The Valentine Street Hustle* is a winner!

As for February... well, I can't resist giving you a peek into next month. Get ready for *Outlaw* by Elizabeth Lowell! Not only is this a *Man of the Month*, it's also another powerful WESTERN LOVERS series.

You know, I could go on and on... but I'll restrain myself right now. Still, I will say that 1991 is going to be filled with wonderful things from Silhouette Desire. January is just the beginning!

All the best,
Lucia Macro
Senior Editor

JEAN
BARRETT

HEAT

SILHOUETTE *Desire*®

Published by Silhouette Books New York

America's Publisher of Contemporary Romance

SILHOUETTE BOOKS
300 East 42nd St., New York, N.Y. 10017

HEAT

Copyright © 1991 by R. L. Rogers

ISBN: 0-373-05617-6

First Silhouette Books printing January 1991

Printed in the U.S.A.

Books by Jean Barrett

Silhouette Desire

Hot on Her Trail #574
Heat #617

JEAN BARRETT

always dreamed of being a successful writer. After much rejection and despair, Jean has attained that dream! Of course, the lucky part is that she has a supportive, patient, loving spouse who was there every step of the way.

A former teacher who has traded the classroom for a typewriter, Jean loves the great outdoors, antiques and cross-country skiing. But she thinks that nothing is more pleasurable than reading.

For two special people,
Jack and Sue

One

Ross McIntyre. The name burned through Anne's mind like an angry flame as the shabby taxi sped her through the nighttime streets toward the Manaus waterfront and a confrontation with the man responsible for her seething frustration.

She recalled the words her head man here in Brazil had used to describe McIntyre over dinner in her hotel less than an hour ago. "This river trader...I think he is very much a law unto himself. Stubborn and independent. A strange breed, even for this region. You understand, I tried in every way to persuade him, but—" he shook his head with regret "—well, he absolutely refuses to take you into the interior, Senhora Richmond. I am sorry, but we must find another way."

A law unto himself. That might be the Brazilian's quaint way of describing Ross McIntyre, but to Anne, he was a callous brute willing to risk a human life by his refusal to carry her upriver with the ransom.

It was a situation she was unwilling to accept. The ruthless people holding her ex-husband, Dane, had been very specific in their instructions about just how she was to reach them with the gold they demanded. There was no other way. Ross McIntyre must be *made* to take her!

The taxi rocked to a stop, indicating her destination. Anne looked through the window, not encouraged by what she saw. They had left behind the sumptuous buildings, the broad mosaic pavements and the modern hotel that had been her only impression of Manaus since her urgent arrival by jet from New Orleans late this afternoon. The squalid harbor district she had been delivered to reminded her that the city was in the very heart of the vast and still primitive Amazon rain forest.

Anne hesitated, experiencing a moment of nervous uncertainty. It had been reckless of her to rush down here like this at night and on her own. The Brazilian would have been horrified if he had guessed this was her intention when she parted from him at the hotel. But her need was a desperate one. If Gabriel Mendes couldn't convince McIntyre to take her on his boat, then she would!

"Senhora?"

The taxi driver had turned and was smiling at her with a mouth full of crooked teeth. He jerked his thumb in the direction of the river to indicate that the vessel she wanted was close by.

Anne stifled her misgivings and leaned toward the driver with renewed determination. "Don't leave. Wait for me right here. You understand?"

The man nodded eagerly. "Yes, yes. It's okay."

The hotel doorman had promised her that the driver fully understood English. She hoped so. She didn't welcome the idea of being abandoned in this questionable place.

She slid from the car, her senses assaulted by rotting odors from the Rio Negro and the mournful twang of a guitar from a nearby cantina. Picking her way over the broken, rough paving, Anne stumbled down to the floating docks made necessary by the fluctuating level of the river.

She found the *Lady Odyssey* on her first try—a snub-nosed, old-fashioned motor yacht that wore the melancholy look of having seen better days. She was a river trader now, her shallow draft permitting her to be berthed close in to the shore.

Except for a single lantern burning on the deck and attracting swarms of enormous moths, the boat was dark and deserted-looking. Summoning her resolve, Anne called out a firm-voiced, "Hello. Anyone on board?"

There was, but when he popped up without warning at the stern rail, she was startled. The man had skin as dark as mahogany on an emaciated frame, his face was pock marked and scarred. One eye was missing, the empty socket cruelly pinched shut, making his countenance a permanent leer.

Anne addressed him in her inadequate guidebook Portuguese. "Senhor McIntyre, *por favor.*"

He regarded her for a moment with his twisted smile, and she feared he hadn't understood her. Then he uttered a brief, *"Sim,"* and pantomiming the act of drinking, pointed back toward the shore and the lighted cantina.

"Obrigado." She tried to thank him, but he had already backed away from the rail and was out of sight.

Anne turned and made her way toward the cantina, the twanging guitar guiding her through the steamy warmth of the night. She almost made her way over the urchin squatting in the dirt just outside the door to the bar. Barefooted and wearing ragged cutoffs, he couldn't have been more than eight or nine, but he was puffing adroitly on a cigarette.

He gazed up at her impishly from a pair of dark, appealing eyes. "You *norte-americano* lady?" he demanded.

She smiled at him. "Yes, I am."

"There is *futebol* there, yes?"

"Futebol?" She did a rapid translation. "Oh, you mean soccer. Yes, we have soccer in North America."

He nodded solemnly. "Someday when I am big I will play *futebol* in that place. Maybe."

"Not if you keep on using those," she cautioned him, indicating the cigarette dangling from the corner of his mouth.

The dark eyes blinked at her in innocence. "Senhor Ross, he doesn't mind and he is from your country."

"No," she said dryly, wondering what kind of man would tolerate a young boy's smoking, "I bet he doesn't."

"Huh?"

"Never mind." Glancing back to assure herself that her taxi was still waiting, Anne stepped regretfully around the little scamp and entered the cantina.

The place was as bad as she expected, smoke filled and dingy, its handful of patrons drinking the fiery rum known as *cachaça*. The guitar went silent with her entrance and she could feel the room's sullen-eyed curiosity. She knew she had no business coming here; she was undoubtedly regarded as an alien and an intruder. She couldn't help that. Steeling herself to ignore the eyes trained on her, she searched the cantina.

There was only one occupant in the room who could be the man she wanted. He was seated at a corner table toward the rear, a bottle of Brazilian beer in front of him. Even from this distance and in the dim, smoky light, Anne could not be mistaken about his identity. His thick black hair and his skin blasted by the tropic sun to the shade of a Brazil nut gave him the coloring of the locals. He was dressed no better than they were in faded jeans and a frayed white polo shirt. But the jeans and shirt hugged a powerfully built body that had obviously been nurtured in a North American climate. There was an attitude in that long, rugged frame that announced a flint-hard nature answerable to no one, and that, too, marked his individuality. Ross McIntyre, owner of the *Lady Odyssey*.

He hadn't noticed her arrival. He was busy sharing his table with a slim, curvaceous young woman who eyed him adoringly as he slipped her a handful of *cruzados*, the Brazilian currency. Anne stiffened in disgust. He was apparently in the act of buying her favors, and she was nearly young enough to be his daughter. But McIntyre's catalog of vices, which seemed to be considerable as Anne was learning at every turn, was none of her business. His boat was.

This was not the moment to interrupt their earnest intimacy, but Anne didn't let that stop her. Head high, ready to do battle, she headed briskly for her objective.

He must have been aware by then of her approach. The girl certainly was and stared at her in wide-eyed surprise. But her companion chose to ignore Anne's appearance at his table until she introduced herself in her low, husky voice. "Mr. McIntyre, I'm Anne Richmond."

He looked up slowly and she saw his face for the first time. Lean-featured and square-jawed, it was a strong, disarming face. A face that had obviously experienced life at its rawest and long ago cast aside all illusions. The face of a cynic.

There was nothing soft nor vulnerable there, not even in the wide, sensual mouth. It was his eyes that were unexpected. She wasn't prepared for them as they met hers from under thick, black eyebrows. They were a clear, smoldering green, and they gazed into her smoke-gray eyes with a challenge that had the air crackling between them.

He was in no hurry to acknowledge her introduction, and when he finally did, it was with a gravel-voiced, lazy insolence. "Anne Richmond, huh? Now why doesn't that surprise me?"

Anne found his cavalier attitude annoying. She hated the loss of self-control he inflicted on her so instantly and so effortlessly. Striving for composure, she made herself go on evenly. "I would appreciate it if we could talk."

Not bothering to stand, he went on considering her for an uncomfortable moment. Then he nodded brusquely and, with his foot on a rung, scraped a vacant chair toward her. "Sit?"

She would have preferred to stand, but feared she would look like a fool. She slid reluctantly into the chair, glancing worriedly at the girl across the fly-specked table.

Ross understood the glance and one of his heavy black eyebrows elevated in sardonic humor. "Rosa doesn't understand a word of English."

Maybe not, Anne thought, but she felt sorry for the girl. Rosa was darting confused, anxious looks from Ross to Anne, sensing the antagonism that still charged the air between them. Antagonism. That's all it was, wasn't it?

Anne, too, suddenly felt confused.

Ross shrugged and with a surprising gentleness leaned over to speak to the girl in fluent Portuguese. She nodded and slipped away from the table. He watched her leave and then turned back to Anne. "Now, Mrs.—"

"Not Mrs.," she corrected him. "Ms., if you don't mind."

"I don't mind at all, but I ought to warn you—that stuff doesn't cut much ice down here."

She shook her head impatiently. "Look, none of that really matters. All I care about is passage on your boat."

"Uh-huh. Well, like I told your gofer this afternoon—"

"He isn't a gofer," she interrupted him again, unable to help her resentment, no matter how much it amused him. "Gabriel Mendes heads a small branch of our pharmaceutical company here in Manaus that happens to be engaged in important research of tropical diseases and the natural rain-forest medicines that might cure them.''

''Real commendable, but it still isn't going to buy you a passage on my boat.''

''May I ask why not?''

''Because a woman like you has no business venturing up into the wild country where you're proposing to go. I would have thought Mendes made that clear to you after our little discussion this afternoon.''

So, Anne thought, bristling, Ross McIntyre was one of those kind, was he? Well, it figured. ''I see.'' She nodded tightly. ''A woman like me. And what is that supposed to mean? Never mind, I know what it is. Spoiled, rich and useless. That's what you're thinking. Well, you're wrong. I may have money, but I earn it in a world which, in its own way, is as tough as yours.''

''Sure. Richmond Pharmaceuticals back in the States, and you're now the top dog of Great-grandaddy's company. Only that happens to be another world from the nasty one where you want to go.'' He lifted the bottle and took a long swig of the beer.

''And you don't think I'm capable of handling it.''

''I know you're not.'' He gestured toward her with the bottle. ''Look at you. No better sense than to come racing down to the rough Manaus waterfront all alone at night and wearing an outfit like that. Aiming to get yourself abused, were you?''

Anne couldn't argue the point. The silk, melon-colored dinner dress was definitely a mistake, but after meeting with Mendes following the arrival of her flight, she had been so frantic that she hadn't waited to change into something more appropriate. Her only thought had been to find a taxi.

''Of course, that wasn't my aim,'' she informed him swiftly. ''The dress was—oh, never mind.''

"What?" He leaned back, rocking slowly on two legs of the chair as he grinned at her wickedly. "Intended for something enterprising along with that sexy perfume you're wearing? Like maybe to seduce me into taking you upriver on my run?"

He was despicable, mocking her again with that raised black eyebrow. Anne held her rage in check with a concentrated effort, her voice softly chill. "I don't want to trade insults with you, Mr. McIntyre, and I'm sorry I need to come to you at all, but there happens to be a human life at stake here."

The front legs of his chair came down hard on the floor. "Right," he said. "The beloved husband."

"*Ex*-husband," she corrected him. "Dane Matthews and I were divorced two years ago."

"But he still counts, is that it? Enough to have you flying down here and hot to rescue him." -

"I had no choice. The instructions specified that I was to deliver the ransom in person, to come without any of my people and to question none of it."

"Did it ever occur to you, lady, that they have law enforcement down here just like back in the States?"

"Involve the police or military in this? You must be joking. Mendes said these people would hear of it in a minute if we tried that, and Dane's life would be worth nothing. I would never risk it."

"That's right," Ross conceded, "your kidnappers aren't very pretty. I've heard of them. Call themselves the People's Liberation Army, but they're more outlaw than political rebel. How did your man come to be grabbed by them anyway?"

"I don't know. I wasn't even aware that Dane was in South America until the phone call came from Mendes yesterday. I heard he was trying to build a career as a free-lance photojournalist. I suppose he may have thought there was a story there.''

"So he just wanders up into their jungle camp, huh? What is it with people like you? You think money is supposed to protect you from everything?''

Anne glared at him. The man was an absolute devil, destroying without effort a composure that had served her faithfully in one of the world's most formidable industries. "Dane has no money of his own," she informed him in a heated rush.

She realized at once that her thoughtless revelation was a mistake. The green eyes narrowed, traveling slowly over her figure. She didn't like what he was thinking nor what he said. "Then it's strictly your dough buying his freedom. Interesting.''

She stirred uncomfortably under his long, intimate gaze. "And what is that supposed to mean?''

"The guy really matters to you.''

"Why? Because I'm willing to pay his ransom?''

"No, because you're so touchy about him.''

"I don't think we need to discuss that aspect of the subject.''

"Okay. Then how about this little aspect? You go up there and since you're the one with the bank account, they grab you and hold you both for a double ransom. You stop to consider that one?''

"That's—that's just something I'll have to risk.''

"Fine. But how can you be sure these people have your ex? What if it's just a setup to have you walking right into their camp? A rich woman all on her own would be a nice catch.''

She shook her head grimly. "There's no mistake. The letter that came to our Manaus office included a photo of Dane in their camp and an added note in his own hand explaining their demand for the gold and what will happen to him if they don't get it."

"A snapshot of tourist with friendly natives, huh? Great. Probably taken with his own camera. Maybe the poor sap even bragged what you're worth and made it easy for them."

Anne gritted her teeth, taking this renegade's unpleasantness because she had no choice. Nothing mattered if only he would help her.

"Now you want to take them a sackful of gold," he went on. "Well, that's just dandy. Ought to buy these *bandidos* a lot more guns and bullets to keep their excuse of a revolution alive. Nice for the innocent along the rivers who suffer for it when the so-called People's Army attacks the shipping and the helpless settlements."

Why was he so angry with her, so sarcastic? Was he simply offended by her money and what he regarded as the privileged air of the rich? Or was there some other private demon gnawing at him? She had never encountered a man like him. He had her trembling with rage.

But there was something more, something far worse. There was his dynamic virility and her growing awareness of it. The excitement of that awareness both shocked and revolted Anne, and she made every effort to reject it, to concentrate on nothing but her mission.

"I—I did think of that," she admitted, keeping a tight rein on her emotions, "and I regret it, but what choice do I have? I can't just let Dane die. I have to pay the ransom. Now, will you reconsider," she pleaded, "and take me upriver on this next run?"

His strong, lean fingers slowly tapped the beer bottle as he gazed at her, the remarkable green eyes stone hard. "Your Gabriel Mendes had my answer," he informed her flatly, "and it still stands. I'm not taking an inexperienced American woman up into that remote territory under these circumstances. It's not just trouble, it's suicide. No way am I having your life on my hands."

She leaned toward him imploringly. "But if I'm willing to risk it—"

"Not on my boat. You want to destroy yourself, you find some other vessel. There are other traders that run the Negro and its tributaries."

"You know that's impossible!" she cried. "These people insist it has to be the *Lady Odyssey*!"

Gabriel Mendes had explained to her why. It was his contention that, because Ross McIntyre and his craft were so familiar and trusted along the rivers, the old yacht could be easily observed in its progress. This would assure the rebels that the enemy in the form of police or military was neither aboard the boat nor pursuing it to their clandestine jungle lair. And, the *Lady Odyssey*'s ability to go where other vessels could not was an added asset.

Ross stirred uneasily under her appealing gaze. "Damn it, woman, you're a headache I never asked for! All right, so maybe it does have to be my boat instead of a nice convenient plane or some other vessel. But that doesn't mean I've got to be responsible for that tender backside of yours. I'll be the carrier, but only for the ransom itself. You'll have to trust me to see it delivered."

Anne shook her head emphatically. "That's out of the question. The instructions insist that I bring the ransom in person, and I'm not going to take a chance on Dane's life by disobeying those orders. I *have* to go upriver myself."

He brought the beer bottle to his mouth and slowly sipped at its contents. All the while, even with his head tipped back, he eyed her. He was silent now, without expression, and she didn't know what he was thinking. The irreverent green eyes gave nothing away, but she could guess at his inner exasperation with her, his unrelenting obstinacy. After all, Gabriel Mendes had more or less gone over the same territory with him just this afternoon, and he hadn't budged then. But this time there was a difference. This time Anne believed she had the means of persuading him to take her aboard his yacht. There was no other way. Before he could voice another negative response, she bent forward. Forcing a low, pleasant voice, she offered him what she hoped was irresistible.

"There's no need for us to go on being unfriendly over this. Not when I can show you how—well, grateful I can be if you'll take me with you."

The green eyes widened, betraying a definite interest. "You want to be friendly? Well, well, who would have figured it." He leaned toward her, his voice turning raspy. "How friendly?"

He understood her. She smiled with satisfaction, her confidence restored now that she knew, in this respect anyway, he was no different from most men. "Whatever you ask," she promised. There was a glitter in the gaze locked with hers and it worried her slightly, prompting her to add a quick, "Within reason, of course."

"Oh, of course," he agreed.

Now what amused him? She could read amusement in his whole attitude. Or was it just eagerness?

"Go on," he coaxed with a slow grin. "Let's get specific."

The hard-bitten features were thrust too close to her own. Anne tried not to let his nearness matter as she answered him. "All right. I know Mendes tried to make it worth your while and you refused. But I'm prepared to be extremely generous. A thousand? Two thousand? Just what will it take?"

He stared at her for a long moment. Puzzled, she watched the green eyes darken like massing storm clouds.

"Money," he said rigidly. "I should have known. You're talking money."

"Naturally. What did you suppose that—" And then Anne realized just what he *had* supposed and her face flamed with indignation. "You're vile! Absolutely vile!"

In one swift, startling movement, the beer bottle in his hand came banging down on the table between them. Anne jumped with alarm, aware of the other patrons in the cantina turning to watch them. Ross, ignoring them, growled a savage, "Sure, that's right! I'm just as rotten as they make 'em! Every corruption in the book! Except for one! This time, all your money doesn't buy you just exactly what you want!"

"Are you saying—"

"Not for sale! Not at any price, that's what I'm telling you!" He pushed back from the table and came abruptly to his feet. Anne, seeing that length unfold for the first time, found there was something awesome in the sinewy male animal suddenly looming over her. "You've got your choice here, Ms. Richmond, and it's your only choice. I take the ransom for you and see it handed over myself, or you find yourself some other carrier. What's it to be?"

Ross McIntyre was a bastard! A heartless, unprincipled bastard! Anne was convinced of it.

She stared up at him in a trembling rage, making a silent promise both to herself and her ex-husband. She might no longer feel anything for Dane except remorse, but she had no intention of abandoning him in his greatest need. To accept McIntyre's offer would amount to abandoning him.

Anne's hand in her lap under the table curled slowly into a tight, determined fist. Ross McIntyre didn't know it yet, but she was going to be aboard his trader when it sailed from Manaus. As a CEO in the highly competitive pharmaceutical industry, there was one thing she had learned. Every man has his Achilles heel, and this man would be no different. She hated the idea of pressuring someone to get what she

needed, but when it involved something so vital as saving a
life and there was no other way...

Yes, she would act because she had to. But the locating of
McIntyre's vulnerability, whatever it was, had better be
quick. According to Mendes, the *Lady Odyssey* was making its next run the day after tomorrow. Well, she had a research branch here in Manaus, didn't she? Now was the time
to see just how good it was.

Anne, refusing to be intimidated, came to her feet and
faced McIntyre coolly. "I don't think we have any more to
say to each other."

He frowned, then nodded slowly. "You made your
choice, huh?"

"That's right. Good night." She turned away and started
to leave the cantina.

"Hey," he called after her. "If you're smart, you'll at
least let me walk you out to the car I assume you've got
waiting for you. This isn't exactly the safest neighborhood,
remember?"

Anne turned, favoring him with a last glance before
shaking her head. "No thanks. It's parked close by."

His broad shoulders lifted in a small shrug. "Suit yourself, then."

She smiled at him wryly. "We spoiled, rich women usually do." Swinging around, she headed again for the door,
slipping past the young boy who was still squatting in the
dirt outside. As exits went, it wasn't a bad one. Except for
one thing. She was still much too conscious of the total sexuality of the man behind her. And considering the swine he
was, she found that awareness unforgivable in herself.

Ross went on standing there, staring after her with a
brooding expression on his angular face. She was gone, but
he was still able to visualize her. He hated himself for remembering that honey-colored hair swinging sleekly to her

shoulders, the smoke-colored, luminous eyes, the elegant figure with a pair of long, silken legs—the kind of legs that should be wrapped around a man. He had encountered other women more beautiful than Anne Richmond, but none with more lush appeal.

It was her voice, though, that stayed with him like a caress. A breathy kind of voice, low and sexy, especially in that moment when he'd been half-convinced she was actually propositioning him, when in spite of himself, he had experienced a heavy stirring in his loins.

Damn, what was he doing to himself? A woman like her. Rich, demanding, wanting her own way no matter what it cost. Her kind was trouble. Hadn't he learned that long ago? *Painfully* learned it?

Ross sank slowly into his chair, reaching for the beer bottle. But he changed his mind and pushed the bottle aside. He didn't want beer. He wanted something stronger, something that was supposed to make you forget. Only he didn't order it. That was another thing he had learned the hard way—that all the whiskey in the world wouldn't cure his black despair. But for a short time, that was exactly how he had tried to combat the nightmare that had ripped through his life. But now he only drank an occasional beer and dealt with the bleakness by avoiding his worst memories of that time as best he could.

A hand touched his arm, and Ross looked up to find Rosa standing at his elbow. She had drifted back to the table and was gazing at him with dark-eyed concern. "Senhor Ross," she asked softly, "there is something wrong?"

He grinned at her ruefully and patted the chair next to him, switching easily to her Portuguese. "Who says? Come on, sit down." She settled in the chair she had occupied earlier, and he leaned toward her. "So, what were we talking about before we got interrupted?"

"Ignacio," the girl reminded him gravely.

Ross nodded. "Right, that little monkey of a brother of yours. Giving you trouble again, I suppose."

"He doesn't regularly attend school," she complained. "I find him in the streets when he should be in the classroom. There are bad influences in the streets, bad temptations. And what am I to do? If we had a father or our mother . . . but we are alone, and I am only a sister and he doesn't listen to me."

"Rosa," Ross gruffly reminded her, "it was a mistake you and Ignacio leaving the mission school and coming down here to Manaus. Sister Veronica tried to tell you that, remember? She tried to warn you that Ignacio was too young and lively, and that he was going to be susceptible to all the wrong elements of a big city after knowing nothing but the forest and the river. You understand?"

Rosa nodded. "It's true, but I wanted a better life for us. I'm not a scholar and there was nothing more the mission school could teach me. There is no opportunity upriver. The only chance for it is in the city. That's why we came to Manaus, so I could work, so that one day Ignacio could attend the university here. He is smart. Everyone says he is very smart, but if I can't trust him to stay in school . . ."

Ross sat back in his chair, long legs stretched out in front of him. "What's all this leading up to, Rosa?"

She bent toward him, her dark, dewy eyes full of appeal. "Take Ignacio with you when you go upriver again. Take him back to Santa Maria do Mato for me. He will be safe with Sister Veronica, and he will learn at the school there until he is old enough to be with me again here in Manaus."

"How the hell did I suddenly turn into this cruise line?" Ross muttered.

Rosa glared at him fearfully. "You—you cannot do this?"

He laughed softly. "Relax, Rosa. I'll take your little monkey back to the jungle for you."

Rosa was all smiles and gratitude. "I will ask a special blessing for you in my prayers, Senhor Ross."

Uneasy with any form of gratitude that might betray his lurking compassion where the poor or helpless were concerned, Ross responded with a quick, rough, "You'd better save your prayers for that brother of yours. Look at him! Mischief looking for a spot to land!" He nodded toward the cantina entrance. Anne had left the door ajar with her swift exit and Ignacio was now poking his head around its edge, curious to investigate a place forbidden to him.

Ross whistled the boy's attention, impatiently waving him over to the table. Ignacio arrived with a grin.

"What are you doing in here, *cavalheiro*? Didn't your sister tell you to wait outside?"

"But, Senhor Ross, you just called me to—"

"Hey, you been smoking cigarettes again?"

Ignacio shook his head. "No, I swear."

"Liar. I can smell it on you. Ignacio, what did I tell you about cigarettes?"

"No good."

"That's right." Ross affectionately poked him in the stomach with his forefinger. "I want your promise, *cavalheiro*. No more cigarettes, and if you behave yourself on my boat, I'll let you take a turn at the wheel."

Ignacio nodded solemnly and promised, but Ross didn't trust the imp. He was too clever.

Rosa opened her purse, producing the money Ross had been pressing on her when Anne arrived at the cantina.

"What are you doing, Rosa?"

"I want to give back something to pay for Ignacio's fare on the *Lady Odyssey*."

"Put it away," he ordered. "There's no charge for Ignacio. That money is to pay for the banana chips."

"But it is too much. I counted it while you spoke to the *senhora*, and it is too much for the order."

Rosa made a living vending a local favorite, fried banana chips. It was a precarious existence and Ross knew she could use anything extra that came her way. "So you give us more banana chips and what Luiz and I can't eat, we'll feed to the fish. Now take Ignacio and get out of here. I'll see you later."

They left him and Ross went on sitting there with his half-finished beer. He knew he ought to be getting back to the boat. His deck hand, Luiz, would be looking for him. They had a heavy day tomorrow. All that cargo for the upriver settlements needed to be hauled aboard and secured. But he couldn't seem to stir himself. He kept thinking about Anne Richmond.

She thought he was a lowlife for treating her so abruptly, real scum for refusing to take her into the bush where she could buy her ex-husband's freedom with her bag of gold. Well, so what? Let her think the worst about him. She was less apt to get hurt that way. After all, he'd offered to carry the ransom for her, to negotiate this guy's release, if necessary. She'd turned him down, so he shouldn't be experiencing any sense of guilt, right? Hell, the rebels might not like it because she had to use some other transport to make contact, but they weren't likely to refuse her gold because of it.

His resistance wasn't because he didn't want to be responsible for her or that he was haunted by the memory of another rich American woman and what had happened to her in the jungle because of him. There was another risk. By taking her aboard the *Lady Odyssey*, he would be advertising to every river settlement along his route that he was helping her to reach the hated rebels. His assistance could be misunderstood. It might destroy his credibility with the suspicious river people and thereby his precious pipeline to all the gossip that seeped into the settlements from the jungle. He couldn't chance not hearing the rumors they shared with him out of trust since one day, there might come to him that scrap of knowledge he lived to hear.

Even so, there had been a moment with Anne when he had weakened. She had trained those beguiling smoke-gray eyes on him and he had almost agreed to take her along, though not in trade for her body as she'd angrily thought. He had been tempted, but not really serious about that side of it. Then she had gone and shoved her fat bank account under his nose and he had come to his senses.

Ross squirmed in self-reproach, willing himself to stop thinking about the danger to this ex-husband of hers. He didn't want to be troubled by any of it, especially her frantic need to save this guy, her eagerness to reach him. Obviously she still cared for him. Why that should bother Ross more than the guilt of his refusal he didn't know. She was nothing to him and he was never going to see the woman again. So what did any of it matter? Well, it didn't. Yeah, then why was he finding it so hard to forget those long silken legs and those soft gray eyes pleading with him?

Two

The blood roared in Ross's ears like wild surf. His long-legged stride carried him angrily across the plush, open-air lobby of the Hotel Fonte with its decorator waterfall and masses of tropical vegetation.

Hell, he might have known she'd be installed in a snooty place like this! Well, he didn't care if she was staying in the Manaus Opera House itself. Whatever the barricades of money and power, he meant to reach her and wring her arrogant little neck. He had never been so enraged.

The wimpy attendant gazed at Ross in horror when he gained the front desk. Ross had been loading the *Lady Odyssey* since sunup, and he looked it—a dark stubble of beard on his chin because he hadn't stopped to shave, his duck pants grimy from handling cargo, large wet circles under both arms of his ratty blue work shirt. He suspected he also bore a pungent aroma, but what did it matter as long as he got his hands on Anne Richmond?

Distaste evident, the clerk asked stiffly, "Can I help you, *senhor*?"

Ross nodded curtly. "You can tell me the room number of one of your guests. The name is Anne Richmond."

The clerk smiled at him in frigid politeness. "I'm sorry, *senhor*. We don't give out room numbers. If you'll let me have your name, I'll call Senhora Richmond's suite and ask if she'll see you."

After what he had been informed of down at the docks this morning, Ross was in no mood for rules. Leaning over the desk, his narrowed gaze meaning business, he addressed the man in a low, lethal voice. "Look, we don't want any unpleasant scenes here, do we? You catch my meaning, *amigo*?"

The young clerk gulped and then reluctantly mumbled the room number.

Ross turned away and headed for one of the glass elevators. He realized that the desk clerk behind him would be leaping for the phone to warn Anne that he was on his way up. So what? He didn't expect or need to take her by surprise. He knew she would see him, especially now that she had the advantage. She would probably enjoy the fact that he was madder than a bull elephant.

As it turned out, his arrival at her door went unannounced. She must have been in the shower and hadn't heard the desk clerk trying to ring her. When she answered his banging, probably thinking it was room service with her breakfast, she was wearing a hastily donned wrapper. She hadn't had the chance to thoroughly towel herself dry and was still slightly damp. The garment clung to her, molded to the womanly curves of her hips and thighs. Ross was suddenly aware that she was braless under the light-weight fabric, her breasts tantalizing in that swollen, unrestrained state. Her honey-blond hair, just shaken out of a shower cap, was tumbled in an appealing way. Without even being conscious of it, she was altogether arousing. That she dared to be so only made Ross more furious with her.

Other than a slight widening of her eyes, Anne registered no surprise over his appearance or his obvious state of displeasure. Come to think of it, she was probably expecting him to show up like this.

"I want to talk to you," he informed her without greeting, his voice hard, biting the words.

One of her damned aristocratic eyebrows arched coolly. "Oh? Is there some problem?"

"No games. I'm not in the mood for them."

She acknowledged his temper with a little nod. "If we're to have a scene, you'd better come in so we can have it in private." She stepped back from the doorway, allowing him to enter a severely modern sitting room.

Ross wasted no time in rounding on her as she shut the door and leaned against it, regarding him with calmly folded arms.

"Lady, you've got some hell of a nerve pulling what you did!"

"You've obviously been told." Her nicely formed shoulders lifted in a little shrug. "As they say, desperate situations call for desperate measures. I'm sorry, but I had to use some means to persuade you to take me upriver, and I was advised this was the only one."

He laughed harshly. "Persuasion? Is that what you call it? I call it a form of blackmail, and a pretty mean version of it at that! Using your pharmaceutical connections to deny kids the medicines they need!" He thrust his face down close to hers as he went on lashing at her bitterly. If he hadn't known better, he might have thought the expression in her eyes was disbelief. "You got any idea in that conniving little head of yours just how much Sister Veronica and her mission depend on the shipments I bring them—the sulfas and antibiotics in a region where diseases are rampant, the vitamins for people whose diets are at a poverty level, the antimalarial and water purification tablets where they haven't heard of sanitation, and, yeah, even the calamine lotion! All the stuff that you arranged with your connections to have withheld from my cargo until I met your selfish demand! Okay, sweetheart, you get your way! You get passage on my boat, but that shipment had better be at the dock this afternoon, *all* of it, or you'll find your pretty little backside swimming upriver with the crocodiles!''

Breathing hard from his hot-blooded outburst, Ross glared at her, challenging her to contradict him. She didn't. Her only visible reaction to his verbal onslaught was a tightening of her folded arms and a low, even, ''Are you through and ready to listen?''

He wanted her explosive indignation, a passion to match his, and all she was giving him was a defiant stare. In her expression he read a smugness that needed to be wiped off her face. Had she been a man, he would have knocked her down. But she was a woman, and there was no way he could touch her, no way he could satisfy what this impotent wildness in him demanded. No way except one.

Had he been in his right mind when he hauled her into his arms, Ross would have realized what a stupid mistake he was making. But he was in the grip of something primal, and it pleased him when those neatly folded arms of hers were no longer secure over her breasts but suddenly pushing against his chest, struggling to break his hold, her head turned away in distaste.

''That's right,'' he whispered savagely, ''I'm an unshaven lout who smells of dirt and sweat, but I'm what you demanded, remember? You'll be on my boat with me for days on end. You'll be in my territory, and you'll take me as I come.''

She faced him in outrage. He seized the opportunity, his mouth swiftly lowering over hers. He meant the kiss to be a quick, hard one, nothing abusive, just a lesson to her. It didn't work that way.

Ross didn't know what happened, but when his lips captured hers, ferociousness deserted him and he found himself devouring her with a raw, all-consuming urgency that had nothing to do with anger and everything to do with desire. He was conscious of her clean, fresh fragrance, the fantastic heat of her flesh under the thin wrapper, and he went crazy, his body thrust against hers, his hand dropping to her hip to strain her against his immediate arousal.

Her plea came to him from under his clinging mouth, a whimper low in her throat. But even as she resisted his assault with a provocative squirming in his arms, he could feel within her a response she was unable to help—a hardening of her nipples against his chest, a parting of her lips that was a sensual invitation. He didn't want it either, this deepening of their kiss, but he was obeying an elemental will stronger than logic when his tongue found its way inside her mouth, probing, stroking, tasting her sweetness.

In the end his emotions couldn't support it. Suddenly hating himself, he released her abruptly. Anne dropped back weakly against the door, mouth swollen, eyes wounded and fierce with accusation.

Ross had achieved what he'd intended—her total resentment. And he wondered why he wasn't feeling satisfied about it.

"Get out!" she whispered, trembling visibly. "Get out of here before I— Just get out!"

He didn't like the way she affected him, either, not during the kiss or now. He didn't like his feelings all in a turmoil. Defenses up, conscience silenced in his old ritual of survival, Ross barked a fast, "The *Lady Odyssey* sails just after sunup tomorrow. If you're not aboard her by then, I leave without you. And don't worry—there won't be any more encounters like that. One more thing. You might be the boss up in your New Orleans executive suite, but on the *Lady Odyssey*, I give the orders. You might see if you can remember that.''

Her reply was to tug open the hall door and to stand aside, silently willing him to leave. He accommodated her, finding his way out to the elevator without a backward glance.

Ross was still in a shaken state, both from the encounter in Anne's suite and the way she had outmaneuvered him to win passage on his boat. When he left the elevator in the lobby, he met Gabriel Mendes, Anne's head man in Manaus.

Immaculate in his tropical whites, the dapper Mendes closed on Ross with smiles and warmth. ''Senhor McIntyre! The very man I need to see!''

In no mood for Latin geniality, Ross responded with a curt, ''What is it, Mendes?''

''I was on my way to Senhora Richmond's suite,'' the Brazilian explained after glancing around to make sure no one was within earshot, ''to inform her that the funds have been converted into the required gold Krugerrands. Not a simple transaction, even with a willing bank.''

''What's your point?''

''Just that the gold will have to be safely stored during the voyage. Senhora Richmond can hardly carry it in her luggage. Is there somewhere secure on your boat?''

''You're in luck, Mendes. We've got a wall safe on board. The *Lady Odyssey* was built for a man who had a need to lock up things. Me, I've never had anything more valuable to put into it than chewing gum.''

The Brazilian was amused by his sarcasm. ''You seem to be in a particularly dissatisfied state, my friend.''

Ross eyed him coldly. ''That so? I wonder why. Think it could be because that boss lady of yours upstairs—who, by the way, made it plain last night she considered me some form of pond scum for turning her down—feels this morning that it's just fine to get her way by holding back a medicine shipment needed for the mission school upriver? Naw, couldn't be that, could it?''

Mendes sighed unhappily. ''That is not quite the whole story, *senhor*. I see I must be fair to Senhora Richmond and explain that my nervous staff didn't...well, shall we say reveal to her either the exact contents of the shipment or its destination. She knew only that it was within our power to withhold a portion of your cargo. Even then, she was reluctant until assured that the cargo would be delivered without delay to those waiting for it. A helicopter was standing by and had you still refused to accommodate her on your boat, the medicines would have been flown upriver and been in your Sister Veronica's hands within a few hours. You see, you mustn't blame her. She thought she was inconveniencing no one but you, and even at that, she disliked doing it. But when a man's life hangs in the balance...''

Ross stared at him in disbelief. The Brazilian nodded slowly. ''It's true. No doubt she was afraid just now to tell you all this herself, fearing then you would fail to keep your word to give her passage. For myself, I know people. I say that, like it or not, Senhor McIntyre would always honor a bargain.''

I'll be damned, Ross thought. There I was misreading her reaction, thinking she was being smug when she was probably shocked over hearing what's in that shipment and where it's going. I didn't even give her the chance to explain.

''Mendes, I ought to break your neck for this.''

He'd made a fool of himself. He'd also been had and he didn't like it. But under his anger stirred a grudging respect for Anne Richmond. Whatever she was, she had grit. He had to give her that. He just wished she wasn't traveling on his boat. She was going to be trouble enough without his having to be reminded every time he looked at her what she had felt like when he had held her in his arms. He was worse than a fool for having tried a thing like that!

I have to survive him somehow, Anne thought nervously as the taxi deposited her close to the dock in the milky predawn light. I don't have a choice about it. I have to board that boat of his, exist with him under strained conditions and close confines, and try to forget what happened yesterday in my hotel room.

The *Lady Odyssey* was waiting for her, floating in the mists off the river, a tramp trader as disreputable-looking as its owner. Rough, offensive. That was Ross McIntyre. It didn't make sense that she was struggling to shake the memory of his kiss, still living with its searing intensity along with the muscled hardness of him, his musky, male aroma, the taste of his mouth on hers. A chemical treachery, a momentary betrayal by her hormones. It had to have been that and nothing more. There couldn't be more with a man like him—a jungle animal alien to her on every level.

You'll get through it somehow, Anne promised herself as she headed resolutely toward the square old yacht. You'll get through it by concentrating on your reason for being here—the need to free Dane from his captors.

There was a figure waiting for her on the dock. To her relief, it wasn't McIntyre but the scarred and hollow-chested deck hand known as Luiz. His dark, homely face wore its contorted smile.

"Bom dia, senhora."

Anne knew just enough Portuguese to realize that he was wishing her a good morning. She returned the greeting as he reached for her only luggage, a sturdy carryall. She surrendered the piece to him and followed him aboard the yacht.

Luiz actually seemed pleased that she was to be their passenger. From his gestures, she understood that he wanted to show her to her quarters. He led the way from the covered teak deck into the spacious aft lounge. With its burnished brass fittings and lavish mahogany paneling, this had obviously once been the pride of the *Lady Odyssey*'s builder. But that had been the elegance of another era. The brass was tarnished now, Anne noticed, the paneling scarred and grimy with neglect, and these days the lounge accommodated cargo. There were piles of it everywhere, and more was stuffed into the forward saloon—stores destined for the settlements along the rivers. Only the galley and dining area tucked behind the raised bridge were cargo-free.

There was no sign of McIntyre anywhere. Anne wondered where he was as Luiz beckoned her down an inside companionway and along a narrow gangway below deck. They passed an unused cabin with more junk in it and then another cabin that was cluttered but reasonably clean. From the glimpse she had of the male clothing strewn on the bunk, she assumed it was occupied by the boat's skipper.

There was still no sign of him as Luiz proudly conducted her into the master cabin at the stern of the vessel, lowering her carryall to the floor and indicating with a wave of his hand that this grandness was to be hers. Anne was touched. The brass had been polished here, the paneling cleaned and rubbed to a soft glow. She knew without being told that it was Luiz she could thank for this effort. The *Lady Odyssey*'s master would certainly never have bothered and, in fact, would probably have preferred his single-man crew to install her in a hammock on the fore deck.

Grinning, Luiz used a bit of the little English he knew. "Nice?"

"Very nice, Luiz. *Muito obrigado.*"

Bobbing his pleasure, he showed her the adjoining head and then departed, leaving her to unpack and settle in. There was very little of that. Anne had wisely brought only the minimum in her carryall. One thing she did want to check on was the wall safe. Gabriel Mendes had informed her last night after delivering the gold to the yacht that it was located in the master cabin.

She found the safe behind an Indian mask and trusted that the gold was secure inside. "Hang on, Dane," she whispered staunchly to the heavy steel combination lock, "I'm coming." However much her ex-husband had hurt her, and he had, she owed him this much—his life. Besides, knowing Dane, there would be no one else he could count on. After she replaced the mask, she washed her hands in the marble basin and found her way topside. Luiz was nowhere in sight. She stood in the thick shadows on the starboard deck and watched the sun about to surface in the east. And where was Ross McIntyre?

She was provided with the answer to that question a moment later when a sorry-looking taxi arrived at the dock and the broad-shouldered figure of the *Lady Odyssey*'s master emerged. He was clad in his familiar uniform of patched jeans, a knit shirt with a seam beginning to part at one shoulder, a pair of scuffed deck shoes without benefit of socks and crammed on his head like a cliché out of an old movie, that dingy skipper's cap. He was everything she didn't admire in a man, down to his robust swagger, and she couldn't forgive her senses for quickening at the sight of him.

She wanted to turn away, to deny his presence, but she was held by the ensuing drama on the dock. Ross wasn't alone. Two other people stepped out of the taxi to join him. Anne recognized them and was surprised. One was the small boy she had encountered outside the cantina, the other, the black-haired girl who had shared Ross's table that night. Gabriel Mendes had mentioned there was currently no woman in McIntyre's life and this girl was so young, but had he spent the night with her? And what was the boy doing with them?

Hugging the deck shadows, Anne was perplexed by a parting scene in a mixture of Portuguese and English.

"All right, Ignacio, say a nice goodbye to your sister, promise her you're going to be an angel for Sister Veronica and tell her you'll study hard and make her proud."

With rolling eyes, the boy obeyed Ross's order, turning to Rosa with a flow of Portuguese. Anne began to understand. There was to be another passenger aboard the *Lady Odyssey*. The boy, Ignacio, was being sent to the mission school upriver.

"Very good," Ross commended him when Ignacio turned from hugging his sister. "Now, *cavalheiro*, before Luiz helps you on board with your gear, let's have the cigarettes you're hiding. No more smokes, remember?"

Ignacio pulled an indignant face, pointing to the two shabby bags the driver had placed at his feet. "Senhor Ross, you searched up all my things when you came for us in the taxi, and Rosa searched them up before that. No cigarettes. I swear it."

"Uh-huh." Ross nodded, smiled down on him and extended his hand. "Well, I'm sorry, monkey, for not trusting you. Let's shake on it."

Ignacio stuck out a grubby hand, Ross gripped it and then in an action so swift that Anne gasped, the boy was lifted with ease into the air, flipped upside down, grasped by the ankles and shaken until he howled. Cigarettes rained on the dock from every little tuck and pocket imaginable.

Anne thought it a humiliating treatment of the boy, but Rosa and Luiz, who had now joined them, were laughing. And Ignacio, who should have been outraged when he had been planted safely back on his feet, grinned up at Ross like an adoring puppy.

Anne found all of it bewildering. This man was determined to bring medicines to a mission, equally determined to free a young boy from a dangerous habit, and neither aim was in character with the Ross McIntyre she had experienced. Had she misjudged him?

She might have been prepared to think so until a moment later when he confronted her. Luiz had taken Ignacio on board to stow his gear and Rosa had departed in the taxi. The sun was just clearing the horizon as Ross looked up from the dock and discovered Anne at the rail. Their gazes clashed with a long potency she didn't care to examine.

His face was expressionless, but she could tell that the hard green eyes were searching her as though hoping for flaws. There was a small, reluctant grunt of approval as he checked out her clothes: lightweight, durable cotton pants, a simple shirt and a wide straw hat in hand for shielding her head from the tropic sun. What had he expected her to turn up in? Designer leisure wear?

Obviously, his hope had been that she wouldn't turn up at all and that the *Lady Odyssey* could sail without her. His attitude said as much and so did his language when all he had to say to her before he swung aboard was a rough, "The *Lady Odyssey* is a working vessel, Ms. Richmond, not a cruise ship, so try to keep out of our way."

That was her only welcome to his filthy boat. She hadn't misjudged him at all. He was foul-tempered and insensitive. She would keep out of his way, all right. She didn't want to be near him any more than he wanted to be near her.

Within minutes, the yacht was underway, chugging out over the broad river under a climbing sun that gilded the dome of the famed opera house the Manaus rubber boom had built a century ago. Anne, standing at the stern rail, watched the city sliding away from them and realized with a grim jolt that she had just sentenced herself to a long voyage with a devil who had her soul in jeopardy.

The suddenness of the jungle was amazing to Anne. One minute there was Manaus, a sprawling, modern metropolis. Then the next, seemingly out of nowhere, there was rain forest. She could find no breaks in the walls of lush, tangled green where liana vines choked soaring trees and giant ferns competed with philodendrons and thickets of bamboo. The brief but brilliant colors delighted her—darting blue morpho butterflies, flashing scarlet macaws, glimpses of yellow orchids. She spotted huge turtles sunning themselves along the fine sand beaches framing the tea-dark river and clouds of insects humming in the lazy heat. Anne found it both beautiful and awesome.

The miles of passing forest were interrupted only rarely by small clearings where primitive settlements hugged the riverbanks. Here, palm-thatched shanties rode on stilts above the temperamental Negro, and from fishing dugouts came the friendly waves of the mestizos and the yapping of their skinny dogs. Anne felt as though a time machine had carried her back to another age.

The larger settlements boasted floating stores with rusty metal roofs, and where these occurred, the *Lady Odyssey* would pause to discharge goods and to take on latex and Brazil nuts gathered from the wild. The stopovers always caused excitement among the locals, who would swarm down to the river's edge to gaze curiously at Anne and to chatter happily to Ross and Luiz as they shifted the loads of goods.

Ignacio cheerfully explained all the passing fascinations to Anne. The boy had attached himself to her and when he wasn't squatting faithfully beside her deck chair in the stern, he was dashing off to the galley to fetch her cool drinks.

Anne laughingly objected to his services. "Ignacio, you mustn't wait on me. I can help myself."

"You don't like attentions?"

"Very much, but not the kind that spoil me. You understand?"

"Sure, I understand. I know English real good."

"You do, and I'm impressed. Where did you learn it?"

"At the mission school. Sister Veronica teaches me. Rosa never learned the English there. Only I did," he boasted.

"And now you're going back to the mission to learn even more, and you and your sister will miss each other."

Ignacio made a face. "Not Rosa. She has Jorge."

"Who's Jorge?"

"Boyfriend. All the time they are kissing faces."

Ross McIntyre was not involved with Rosa, Anne realized. Apparently, he was simply helping the girl and her brother. She wished she could really believe in the man's humaneness, but this was difficult in the face of his treatment of her.

He had commanded her to keep out of their way, meaning *his* way, and Anne strove to do just that, but it was a hopeless effort on the small yacht. He was like a restless jaguar, forever turning the helm over to Luiz so he could prowl the decks with his impatient, energetic stride. Wherever she settled, it wasn't the right spot. He would be there, glowering at her as he reached around her to check a cable or a fitting on a hatch. He would grumble darkly if she didn't move aside quickly enough. He would look surly whenever Ignacio or the kindly Luiz paid her any small attention.

He resented her, of course, angry not just with her presence on board, but with the knowledge that he had been made to have her here. Well, she, too, regretted the necessity of having pressured him. If his black mood ever lifted long enough, she intended to apologize. Maybe she could even convince him she was a decent person who hated that circumstances had necessitated her action.

Meanwhile, the tension was mounting between them. Whenever he snapped at her—and yes, that too, happened as the day wore on—she found herself struggling with the childish longing to push him overboard. There was no doubt about it. The man had a talent for bringing out the worst in her.

Then why, heaven help her, was she so aware of him? Why did she keep on noticing such disturbing things about him—the shadow of his beard on his stubborn jaw, the film of perspiration in the hollow of his tanned, strongly corded neck, the way his powerful thigh muscles rippled sensuously in his snug jeans when he moved along the deck?

This man shouldn't be sexy, Anne thought in a panic. By every definition of what she had always considered appealing in a male, Ross McIntyre had no right to his sexiness. There was too much of him—too much solid height, too much black, curling hair on his forearms and at the open collar of his shirt, too many sharp angles on his lean face, too much force in his gruff voice. Too much of everything but the sensitivity she prized in a man. Then why couldn't she control her awareness of him? And how was she supposed to stand the long upriver haul in his close company?

It was not knowing where it would all end that frustrated her. The rebels holding Dane had no intention of revealing the location of their camp until they were ready to do so. She could do nothing but wait until they contacted her with further instructions, and this might not occur until the *Lady Odyssey* was far into its run. Days from now. In the meantime, there was the winding river and the steaming jungle. And there was Ross McIntyre and her frightening inability to escape his growing effect on her.

The *Lady Odyssey* was anchored for the night off one of the river's countless islands. Down in his cabin, Ross was washing up for the supper that Luiz was putting together in the galley. It had been a long day and he was exhausted.

He was reaching for a towel when he caught sight of his face in the mirror above the basin. He stood there for a long moment, considering his reflection. He didn't like what he saw. He was scowling. He realized that there had been too much of this lately. Too many difficult moods, too many bad tempers. He couldn't go on like this. Much more and he wouldn't be able to live with himself.

Why kid himself, though? He knew why he was frowning, why it had been a strenuous day. It was because *she* was on board his boat. Not just on board—but everywhere. He couldn't turn around without seeing that slim, shapely figure leaning on a rail or hearing the low, husky laugh as Ignacio entertained her. Worse, her gaze followed him. The smoky eyes with their thick, dark lashes tugged at his senses even though they looked at him reproachfully.

She thought he was still fuming because she had forced him to take her upriver, that he was determined to make her pay for her tactics. She didn't know that his irritable mood was a defense against her attractions. He wanted her. It didn't make sense and he was living in hell for it, but he wanted her. He had since that first night she had walked into the cantina, even if he hadn't admitted it to himself until now.

He wasn't going to do anything about it, though. He'd be the biggest fool even to try. After all, there was a worse hell than the enticement of Anne Richmond, and it was with him every hour of every day. The raw wound of a tragedy that might never be healed. The destruction of his world because of a headstrong woman with money and influence.

All right, so maybe it wasn't fair to treat Anne as though she were another Claire, to resist her very image just because she came from that same sphere of wealth and power. But he wasn't going to chance it. He couldn't afford to when the tragedy was unsolved, when he was still searching for a resolution to it somewhere out there in the jungle. He might never find it, but he wouldn't stop trying.

He was still frowning in the mirror. What was it now? Anne again, of course. To be honest, it bothered him that she thought he was an insufferable bastard. But wasn't this way better for both of them? As long as she felt like that, it would keep them apart. Anything else with two such opposing forces was bound to mean trouble.

Besides, he was forgetting that there was the ex-husband. The guy must still mean a lot to her or she wouldn't be going to such lengths to rescue him. Damn, he had to stop minding about that. He had to detach himself from the whole thing.

The others were waiting for him when Ross arrived in the dining area. He started to join them at the table when he noticed the place settings. What was going on here? Where were the old plastic dishes they always used? This stuff looked like fine china.

Ignacio was eager to explain. "Luiz brought the dishes from where they were stored years ago. They are from the days when the boat was a fine yacht. Luiz thought it would be good to use them again."

"Oh, he did, did he?" They weren't fooling him. The china that he hadn't even known existed had obviously been dragged out and polished in order to please the woman sitting across from him. She was turning his comfortable old tub into a cruise ship. How did she do it? Ignacio had been stumbling over himself all day to run and fetch for her. Now she had Luiz at her feet.

She surprised him with her anxious, "I'm sorry. I had no idea Luiz was going to all this trouble."

Ross said nothing as he settled in his chair, but he noticed everyone breathing small sighs of relief over his acceptance. All right, so maybe he had been unfair. Maybe it was time he started to be polite to her. He could offer that much without risk, couldn't he?

Picking up a steaming platter of fish, Ross passed it to Anne with a pleasant, "You ever try pirarucu? It's a favorite down here. I think you'll like it."

He caught Luiz and Ignacio exchanging disbelieving glances. He ignored them and concentrated on being civil.

Ross's politeness lasted until the next day. He went into the lounge to search for a misplaced tool when he noticed smoke drifting up from behind the stacks of cargo. His suspicion was confirmed when he slipped around the piles and caught Ignacio hiding on the floor with a tin can in his lap and a lighted cigarette in his mouth.

Ross snatched the cigarette out of the boy's mouth and crushed it in the can before he hauled Ignacio to his feet. "We cleaned you out of every last one of those things! So, where did you get it? No lies this time, either! I want the truth!"

Ignacio, choking on the smoke he'd swallowed when Ross had surprised him, struggled to answer him. "The *Lady*—" He coughed and tried again. "I got it from the *Lady*—" He was unable to go on.

Ross had heard enough. Predictably, his temper flared. There was only one "lady" on board this boat, and she was going to hear from him! Turning on his heel, he headed for the stern deck where Anne had settled after lunch. She didn't know it yet, but they were about to be engaged in another head-on collision!

Three

Anne had brought a folder of essential work from her New Orleans office. In this setting and with circumstances being what they were, she wasn't having much luck concentrating on the market survey occupying her lap. She had removed her reading glasses and was returning the report to the folder when she saw Ross bearing down on her from the direction of the lounge.

One glimpse of those flashing green eyes and that pugnacious jaw told her they were about to have another confrontation. Oh, Lord, what now? she wondered.

Ross's voice was like gravel. "I have something to say to you."

Anne rose from the deck chair, bracing herself. "What happened to last night's courtesy?" she asked. "Or did I just imagine it?"

He looked hot enough to blister, snarling a rough, "I'm not like you executive types, Richmond. I don't go around being polite with people who are sneaking behind my back."

"No, you just go straight for the throat. What do you mean, sneaking behind your back? What are you accusing me of now?"

"You tell me. I've got a kid back there hooked on tobacco. I'm trying to unhook him. I made sure he didn't have a single cigarette on him when he came aboard. And yet he was smoking one just now in the lounge."

"And you think that I—" Anne fought for self-control, though she was trembling with indignation. "Why? Why me?"

"Because Ignacio swears you gave him the cigarette, and this time he's too scared to lie about it."

"I don't care what he says. It isn't true. And how dare you go and assume I would provide a child with cigarettes. Or anyone, for that matter. And since I don't smoke and never have, where do you suppose I'd even come by cigarettes?"

"How the devil do I know what your habits are?"

"Oh, I see. You think I keep a supply of the things to hand out—like little tips."

"It might explain why Ignacio has been running and fetching for you ever since you came on board. I imagine women like you are used to errand boys."

Anne wasn't conscious of her arms winding across her breasts, her hands hugging her sides. It was an instinctive, self-protective gesture she had acquired when she had been married to Dane. She had frequently needed the defensive stance in those years. The habit had stayed with her, surfacing in especially hurtful moments like this one. She recalled how Ross had observed it the morning he had stormed into her hotel suite but he had misunderstood it. There wasn't anything that he did seem to want to understand about her, and she told him as much.

"Yes, Ignacio has been trying to please me, whether I wanted him to or not. And so has Luiz. It doesn't take bribery, either. All it takes is a little kindness. You might try it yourself. You'd be surprised at how far it goes. Now, if you don't mind, I'd like myself cleared of this wild charge you've leveled at me.''

He scowled at her blackly for a moment, then turned his head, bellowing an insistent, "Ignacio, get out here!"

The boy, hanging at the open lounge door, had been expecting the summons. He crept toward them sheepishly. Ross's gaze, meeting his, meant business. "All right, monkey, did you or did you not tell me that Ms. Richmond gave you the cigarette?''

Ignacio gulped before whispering a quick, "Not.''

Ross frowned at him severely. "You were lying again, even after—''

"No lies!'' Ignacio shook his head emphatically, then rushed to explain. "I tried to say it right, but the smoke went down bad when you caught me, and then you didn't stop to listen, Senhor Ross. I tried to say I got the fag from the *Lady*—''

"Ms. Richmond.''

"No, *this* lady," he said impatiently, his bare foot stomping the deck. "The boat lady.''

"The *Lady Odyssey*? What the heck does that mean?'' Ross stared at him disbelievingly.

"That seat thing in the lounge—''

"The banquette?''

"Yes, that thing with the cushions. I was looking under the cushions for the coins the people maybe lost from their pockets when they sat there.''

"And you found an old cigarette?''

"Yes, an old cigarette. From the *Lady Odyssey* lounge. That is what I was wanting to say.''

Anne's eyes met Ross's as she demanded bluntly, "Doesn't that temper of yours ever stop to think before it acts?''

He said nothing for a full minute, but his face was a study in shifting moods: soberness, then actual embarrassment, and finally remorse. When he opened his mouth at last, Anne thought he was going to offer an apology. She was startled by his low, somber, "Don't give up on me."

She wasn't sure whether the words were directed at her, Ignacio or the world in general. She could sense it was the plea of a man struggling with some private torment, and its poignancy strangely touched her.

She could see that Ross found his remark unexpected. He shook his head, as though in denial. Then, without a word of explanation, he turned on his heel and strode off toward the bridge.

Anne watched him go in bewilderment. Even now in this strained moment, she was aware of the retreating figure exuding a powerful male sexuality. She didn't understand it. How could he go on affecting her like this when, from the moment she had met him, they had been circling each other like wary adversaries?

You're in the tropics, Anne reminded herself. You have to expect it to be hot.

But this acknowledgment in no way helped her late-night sleeplessness. She had gone to bed believing herself to be tired, but the stale, sultry air below deck had kept her awake, turning restlessly on the damp sheet.

She shouldn't be blaming just the heat, though. After all, she was used to the steaminess of New Orleans in midsummer, and this was no worse. There was something else responsible for her fitfulness. In fact, two somethings. The man in the cabin next to hers and the man waiting for her somewhere upriver.

There was no use lying here like this, she decided. She would only spend the rest of the night wearing herself out with a lot of fretting over what she couldn't help. The thought of the open deck overhead and the possibility of cooler air beckoned her. Leaving the rumpled bed, she slipped into jeans and a loose top.

The cabin adjoining hers was silent, its door was closed as Anne passed it on tiptoe, refusing to think about the man behind it. A night lamp burning at one end of the narrow gangway guided her topside.

There, the air was warm but less heavy. Anne made her way through the lounge and out on deck, planning to settle in her favorite spot in the stern, but a pair of hammocks had been strung there below the canopy. The snoring coming from under the mosquito nets draped over them indicated that Luiz and Ignacio had settled there for the night. Anne knew that Luiz had his own quarters below deck somewhere near the forward saloon. Most evenings, though, he wisely chose to sleep in the open.

She decided to try the forward deck. The *Lady Odyssey* creaked softly at her moorings as Anne turned and made her way along the rail. She was surprised when she neared the bow. She wasn't alone here, either. Ross's tall, compelling figure stood at the rail, etched in profile by the white light of a hazy half moon. So he, too, wasn't able to sleep.

Anne didn't want any more unhappy encounters with him. She would have turned away and crept back to her cabin, but she was struck by his attitude. He wasn't aware of her hanging in the shadows. His mind was clearly elsewhere as she watched him for a moment, deeply puzzled by the direction of his gaze.

They were anchored for the night in a mist-washed cove, the nose of the yacht pointed toward the thick mass of the jungle. Ross was searching the dark trees on shore. He wore an expression of quiet desperation that tugged at her heart. Her reaction to his bleakness was similar to the one she had experienced this afternoon. Again it surprised her.

Suddenly, she was regretful. Obviously this was a private moment, and she was trespassing. She started to back away when he spoke to her without turning his head. His deep voice was unexpectedly friendly.

"You don't have to leave."

Anne hesitated, but he seemed to be waiting for her. Not wanting him to think she was spying on him, she joined him at the rail with a quick explanation. "I couldn't sleep. It was hot in my cabin. I thought it might be cooler out here."

He nodded understandingly. "Yeah, I know what that's like. Insomnia and I are old friends."

"The heat?"

"No, that doesn't bother me. I'm used to the climate down here. I almost thrive on it."

She glanced up at his dark profile. The moonlight emphasized the sharp ruggedness of his features, carving strong masculine angles and planes. The twin grooves that were cut from his nostrils to the sides of his mouth were more shadowed, too. Care lines.

Anne waited for an explanation of his insomnia. He didn't offer one. She wondered if his sleeplessness, the care lines on his face and the private demon that seemed to rule him were all connected with the same thing. Maybe they had to do with what he had been looking for in the forest.

She turned her head, gazing off into the jungle. What did he search for out there? What did he want to find? Or was she just being fanciful? It would be easy to let her imagination govern her thoughts on a night like this. The moonlight captured the senses, making magic out of the ordinary. Fireflies, like tiny green lanterns, starred the shoreline against the dense lacework of vines and trees. There was the flutter of bats, the restless night sounds of the teeming jungle, the lap of water against the hull, the mysterious odors of river and forest.

"It's beautiful, isn't it?" she observed. "Primitive but still beautiful."

"It can be when it's like this," he agreed. "It makes you forget just how deadly the jungle is."

"But not spoiled."

"Well, not here anyway. Not yet. But south of the Amazon, it's another story."

"Yes, I've heard how they're exploiting the jungle there."

He made no comment. She was conscious of his gaze lingering on her and she felt vulnerable. She didn't understand him. He was so different tonight. His voice didn't carry that caustic note that perpetually sounded as though he had an old score to settle. His eyes were neither mocking nor challenging her. His impatient energy had softened into an actual gentleness. The new mood from this mercurial man made Anne more nervous, however, than his daylight anger.

She found herself covering her awkwardness with small talk. "Where are the mosquitoes? I thought they would be thick out here."

Ross had turned to face her. His long body was leaning against the rail in a relaxed stance. He smiled down at her in amusement, and she knew he understood her sudden apprehension. But it was an easy amusement with nothing sarcastic in it.

"It's the dry season," he explained. "Also, there are fewer mosquitoes along the Negro. They tell me it has something to do with the chemistry of the waters."

"Oh."

A breath of air stirred over the river, and the *Lady Odyssey* sighed again at her cables.

"She's a tramp," he said. "Like me. Maybe that's why we get along so well together."

"Who?"

"The boat."

"Oh," she said again.

He was still watching her with that lazy smile. He seemed to have forgotten his preoccupation with the jungle. Anne wondered why she felt compelled to go on standing here close beside him, why she wasn't retreating from a situation that was making her increasingly light-headed.

She's nervous with me, Ross thought. He didn't blame her, not after the way he had been treating her. But he didn't want her to be uneasy. Not tonight, not in this moment. He wanted her to trust him, and he didn't know why. It was probably the damn moonlight, which had penetrated all his careful defenses, making him aware of her tantalizing femininity.

He couldn't seem to see anything but the moonlight kissing her silky blond hair. Couldn't smell anything but the arousing fragrance of her near flesh. Couldn't hear anything but the husky cadence of her sexy voice.

He had no business touching her. It was something he shouldn't even have considered trying. But it happened before he could stop it. Moonlight was never ruled by logic. All it did was bewitch you.

He found his hands framing her face, his thumbs slowly stroking her features. She had a delicate bone structure, a fragility that he was convinced belied an inner strength. But she wasn't being strong now. She was trembling under his hands and her vulnerability awakened in him a rush of male protectiveness that struck him forcefully in the vitals.

It didn't make sense. None of it made sense. It was as astonishing as the fact that she let him touch her at all, that she hadn't backed away when he had moved close. The moonlight again. It was affecting her, too. He could see it shimmering in those wide, thick-lashed eyes searching his. Pensive gray eyes that had him wondering what was going on behind them. What was she thinking? Feeling?

He knew what *he* was feeling, all right. His blood was as hot and heavy as the jungle. His senses hummed, all of them vitally alive. He was obeying the throbbing sensuality of a tropical night, not his own reason or will. He knew that, and he didn't care. He had to kiss her.

Still framing her face, Ross brought his mouth down to hers. He made it a tender kiss, not like that pagan business in her hotel suite. He didn't want to hurt her. He wanted to guard her. She sensed that and accepted his lips. And then he learned what Anne, herself, was feeling. There was a sizzle answering his as their tongues met in her mouth, a wild, slashing something that threatened to destroy the gentleness he intended.

For a moment, though, Ross surrendered totally to the molten urgency that was between them as he eagerly explored the sweet depths of her mouth, his tongue playing with hers in a fiery dance. Her body sagged weakly against him, pressed willingly to the hardness she had instantly ignited.

The kiss grew even more intimate, more abandoned as his spearing tongue made its man-hungry demands inside her mouth. She tasted of a heat and a desire that had his insides churning with a mindless passion. He could feel her swollen breasts against his chest, the tightening of her nipples through the thin fabric of her shirt. She clenched at him, her body welcoming the slow, grinding thrusts of his pelvis against her softness.

Much more of this, he realized, and they would both be beyond the point of self-control. He didn't want the regrets and the guilt that were bound to follow, neither his nor hers. It took all his will to drag his mouth from hers, to release her. Visibly shaken, she leaned back against the rail, supporting herself.

He was right. He could read the shock in her face over the intensity of her response to his kiss. She hadn't wanted this to happen any more than he had. They couldn't afford each other. Their worlds were too far apart.

Her voice was ragged and breathless, struggling to recover. "I—I think I'd better get back to my cabin."

She was running away. He tried not to mind that, to see it as a sensible intention. He forced himself to reply with an ordinary, "There's a fan in one of your lockers. I think it still works. It might let you get back to sleep."

Anne shook her head. "It wasn't just the heat that kept me awake," she confessed anxiously. "It's all this nervous waiting for the rebels to contact us. I know I have to be patient, but I keep wondering . . . well, just when and where it will happen."

You're a fool, McIntyre, he told himself harshly. You let a lot of hokey tropical moonlight go to your head, probably just like it went to hers. Because all she really cares about is reaching this ex-husband of hers. That's all she ever wanted.

He tried to keep the bitterness from his voice when he answered her. "Don't worry. The rebel connections are watching us, you can bet on it. They know just who we are and where we are, and the grapevine out there in the bush is letting the rebel camp know it, too. When they're sure of us and the time is right, they'll make the contact. Then you'll get your reunion with the hotshot photojournalist."

Anne stared at him, stung by his scorn. Why had he shut down on her again? Why these wild swings in mood? She had no business reaching out to him, but she sensed he was hurting and she wanted to help.

"You're angry with me," she said. "Is it because I—"

"What?"

"Well, I couldn't help noticing how you were watching the jungle when I came on deck. You were so intense about it, and if I've intruded on something—"

"You haven't."

"Don't misunderstand, but if you should want to talk about it—"

"You'll lend a sympathetic ear. Thanks, I appreciate the offer, but you've already got a man you're helping. Isn't one enough?"

Another snide reference to Dane. Is that how he read her frustration over this long voyage? Thinking that she was eager to be with her ex-husband and wild over the delay?

She considered trying to make him understand that her only need in securing Dane's release was to put something unpleasant behind her. But Ross didn't want her explanations. He resented her, and she could tell that he regretted his momentary weakness as much as she did.

No more encounters like that, she promised herself. Whatever his sexual attractions, he isn't for you, Anne.

She abruptly left him, moving off toward her cabin. She thought he would let her go without another word, but when she reached the lounge door, he called out a dispassionate, "We'll be arriving at the mission school tomorrow. Just so you know that we are getting somewhere on this run, even if it's not where you want to be."

Anne turned, expecting him to be grinning at her vilely. But he was facing the jungle again with that forlorn expression on his lean face. She gazed at him for a moment and was struck by a sudden, disturbing realization. Why hadn't she seen it before? That under the bearish temper and macho virility was a very lonely man.

Santa Maria do Mato—Saint Mary of the Forest—was located on a point of land near the confluence of the Rio Negro and the Rio Jara. Anne was standing on the forward deck as the *Lady Odyssey* approached the mission school late the following morning. She saw a collection of palm-thatched structures that was no more imposing than any of the settlements they had stopped at along the river. But she did notice one difference—the place was scrupulously neat and clean.

As the yacht slid toward the floating dock, a grinning Luiz announced their arrival from the helm by sounding the boat horn. The deep hooting startled Anne and delighted two dozen barefooted children, who raced out of an open-sided shelter and came shrieking down to the shore to welcome them. The arrival of the *Lady Odyssey* was apparently an exciting event.

Anne witnessed a surprising scene from her position at the rail. As Ross sprang to the dock to secure the lines, the children swarmed around him. They tugged at him familiarly, hopped up and down and shouted for *chicle*. From his bulging pants pockets he dispensed the chewing gum they demanded, listened sympathetically to a woeful tale about an unfair soccer match, and placed his ridiculous skipper's cap on a little girl's long, black hair. It came down over her ears and her eyes. She loved it.

They all loved his attentions. And for the first time since Anne had met him, Ross was thoroughly enjoying himself. The man is a walking contradiction, she thought in wonderment.

He must have sensed her watching him. For a brief moment, his laughing gaze met hers, jolting her with the unexpected contact. His eyes turned sober. Was he communicating a silent apology for last night? She didn't know. The man was too complicated for her to read him accurately.

The moment was gone when Ignacio appeared at her side, asking her to help him ashore with his gear. Anne obliged. By the time they got down to the dock, a woman with short, graying hair and a sturdy figure in blue jeans and T-shirt was wading through the commotion with a robust, "So help me, McIntyre, if you don't stop destroying my morning lessons with that boat whistle, I'm going to scuttle this old tub of yours! Well, where is he?''

"Here I am, Sister!" Ignacio announced his presence from Anne's side.

It was then that Anne noticed a small, silver cross on a thin chain over the woman's T-shirt and realized this was the only traditional badge that identified Sister Veronica.

The nun worked her way to where they were standing at the edge of the crowd, clapping Ignacio affectionately on the backside. "So, you little scamp, you're back with us, huh?''

Ignacio grinned at her. "Yes, Sister. This is my friend, Senhora Richmond. She is pleased if you call her Anne.''

Anne and the nun exchanged amused glances. "Welcome to Santa Maria, Anne." Sister Veronica offered a firm handshake.

"You were expecting Ignacio," Anne realized in surprise.

"We're remote here, but not that remote. We have a two-way radio. Manaus informed us he was coming. You, too.'' If Sister Veronica had been told the reason for Anne's voyage upriver, she tactfully refrained from saying so.

The nun took charge of the situation, directing one of the older boys to her side. "Ramirez, you help Ignacio get his things up to the dormitory and see he gets a bed. Not next to Mo, either. If I remember rightly, they hate each other's guts. We'll have to work on that. McIntyre, I'm taking Anne on up to the porch for a cool one. She has better sense than to want to go on standing out here in this sun.''

Ross offered no response. He was still involved with the children. Sister Veronica shook her head blithely. "He's not paying any attention to me. He never does. Come on," she urged Anne. "They'll be fooling around like this forever before they get around to unloading my goods.''

She joined the nun. They left the noisy dock and started across the clearing. When Anne expressed interest in the community, Sister Veronica pointed out the structures. "Boys' dormitory on this side, girls' over there. That's the classroom in the center. Kitchen and dispensary down there."

Anne paused at the open door of a small, plain building not yet identified. Glancing inside, she saw benches and an altar. "Your chapel, I take it."

The nun nodded proudly. "You ought to hear the kids when they fill it with song. Of course," she added regretfully, "we have to manage our music *a cappella*. One day, when Santa Maria can afford it, I hope to install a spinet piano."

Anne turned to her, bemused. "Sister, you don't operate this whole setup here on your own, do you?"

"Oh, we manage all right. The kids are great, and I have an older woman who cooks and a younger one with some nurse's training. A traveling priest comes by once a month in his dugout to say Mass and hear our confessions, and a doctor with a dubious reputation calls around when I need him. Of course, they're both scandalized by the way I dress and by my methods. And it's true. I should be altogether interested in the souls of my charges, and I find myself at times more interested in their physical welfare. The people down here lack so much."

"But you're so far away from everything."

"That's the point, you see. Some of the kids are locals, but most come out of the *favelas*—slums, that is—in places like Manaus. Here in the wilderness, away from the influences of the gutters, they stand a chance."

Anne had nothing but admiration for the nun and her efforts.

Minutes later, she was installed in a basket chair on the shady porch of Sister Veronica's quarters, sipping pineapple juice that had been chilled in an ancient gas refrigera-

tor. The refrigerator shared one end of the porch with a
mangy-looking parrot asleep on his perch.

Anne found the nun easy to talk to, probably because
Sister Veronica had such a natural empathy. She expressed
interest in Anne's work. "Manaus mentioned you operate
a pharmaceutical company back home. Does that make you
a scientist?"

"Far from it, although I have acquired enough biotech
knowledge to make me effective during product develop-
ment meetings with our labs and sales force. I also have a
useful marketing expertise. Right now," she added with
pride, "we're investigating ways to make medications and
vaccines more affordable to underdeveloped countries."
Regions like this one, Anne thought, and made a mental
note to herself to make her company's resources available
to Sister Veronica.

The nun's blue eyes sparkled with good humor. "Sounds
like you have the same busy existence I do. What do you do
with yourself when you're not running your business?"

The question was casual and friendly, but Anne realized
she had no satisfactory answer for it. What *did* she do with
herself outside of Richmond Pharmaceuticals? She was involved in funding for the preservation of the historic New
Orleans she loved, and when her schedule permitted, she
enjoyed cooking creole dinners for friends. Yes, she filled
her life and all her pursuits were worthwhile ones or she
wouldn't be undertaking them, but they suddenly seemed so
inadequate. "Nothing very special, I'm afraid," she hedged.

"No family?" Sister Veronica probed gently.

Anne shook her head. "Not close family. Not anymore." It was true, she realized. There was no one currently with whom to share her existence. Until this moment,
it hadn't seemed to greatly matter, maybe because she had
been too busy to stop and consider it. But right now she felt
there was a noticeable gap in her life.

Down across the clearing, the children were enjoying the recess from their morning lessons. All of them watched in fascination as the two men unloaded supplies for the mission school. Even from this distance, Anne was disturbed by the rangy figure sweating beside Luiz, his muscles bulging as he shifted the heavy cartons.

Sister Veronica, noticing where her gaze was lingering, asked thoughtfully, "How are you and McIntyre getting along?"

Anne was sure that the nun didn't intend her question to be in any way connected with what they had just been talking about. Even so, she didn't find the subject a safe one. She answered Sister Veronica reluctantly but with honesty. "We're not. He's exasperating."

The nun slouched in her chair and chuckled deeply. "That's our Ross. Patience and tact are definitely not among his virtues."

"Not with me, anyway. I'm afraid he resents my being aboard the *Lady Odyssey*. In fact, he resents me, period."

Sister Veronica surprised her with a mystifying, "Oh, I don't imagine it's you he resents personally, Anne, but what he feels you represent."

"I don't understand."

"No, and it isn't my place to tell you, but people do misjudge Ross. He doesn't let them get close, so they have no way of knowing that he carries an awful burden. He wouldn't thank me for explaining something that's private and very sensitive, and that's why I won't betray his confidence by trying it now. I would just like you to know he isn't what he seems."

Another enigma, Anne thought. "What is he then, exactly, Sister?"

The nun sighed. "A man who is hurting deeply, I'm afraid, and with good reason. But when men like Ross hurt, they hit back. It's just their way, right or wrong."

"Yes, I've been the target of that temper of his."

Sister Veronica smiled. "Well, I won't say he isn't mean when he's provoked. A man has to be tough to survive down here, Anne, particularly in his business. But under the roughness, I think there's a real compassion. He just doesn't easily relate it."

Anne wasn't convinced. A man could be strong without being hard. How could she possibly believe him compassionate or vulnerable when every time she tried to see a better nature in him, he would deny her effort with his nastiness? But then, she remembered the children. "He does have a soft spot for kids, anyway, doesn't he?"

"Well, of course, he would have."

"What does that mean, Sister?"

"Nothing," the nun said carelessly, but Anne wondered if her puzzling remark had been another reference to the mystery about Ross and his alleged burden.

"I just meant," Sister Veronica went on quickly, "that it isn't only young people he cares about in that way, though he pretends otherwise. It's anyone who isn't big enough or strong enough or rich enough to help himself. Luiz is a good example of that."

"His deck hand?"

"Employment down here is hard enough to come by for men who are healthy and whole, and with Luiz's disfigurement and a body like a skeleton . . . well, Ross took him on when no one else would. Even tried to teach him some of his civil-engineering skills, but I'm afraid in that department Luiz is—"

"Wait a minute, Sister," Anne interrupted her. "Are you telling me that by profession Ross McIntyre is a civil engineer?"

"I guess you wouldn't have any reason to know that."

"But then why . . . ?"

"What?"

Anne shook her head.

"Oh, I see," the nun realized. "You wonder why he's buried himself in a backwater like this, why he runs the rivers in that derelict old boat instead of practicing his profession."

"It isn't a very ambitious existence, is it? If he is interested in helping people, it seems to me that, as an engineer, there are better ways and better places for helping them."

Sister Veronica crossed her ankles and slouched even lower in her chair. "Just like people, Anne, things aren't always what they seem. And, of course, you don't understand what I'm trying to say. But, again, I can't explain. I've already said way too much, and if I say anything more, that long drink of water headed our way is going to have me for lunch."

Since Ross was, in fact, striding across the clearing toward them, the conversation had to be left frustratingly unfinished. He stopped below the porch, hands stuffed into his jeans pockets, the skipper's cap back on his head and at a rakish angle. He gazed at them suspiciously, as if he guessed the subject of their discussion and didn't care for it.

Sister Veronica, without a trace of guilt, waved the jug of pineapple juice toward him. "Interested?"

"Not unless it's cold beer."

"McIntyre, you know I don't keep beer in my fridge. Not that occasionally I wouldn't mind one myself if I didn't have twenty-five cherubs on the premises. Everything unloaded?"

"And under cover." He shifted his weight restlessly and glanced at Anne. She got the message. He was wearing the look of wanting to talk privately to the nun.

Anne left the chair and wandered to the far end of the porch on the pretext of visiting the parrot. The bird had awakened on his perch. He was an irascible creature, croaking something unfriendly in what she assumed was Portuguese.

She could feel Ross's eyes following her as he joined Sister Veronica on her side of the porch. Anne thought she was far enough away not to overhear them, but she couldn't help catching the communication between them, soft though it was.

"Anything new from the bush?" That was Ross's deep voice.

The nun's reply was grave. "Not anything you want to hear. Sorry, Ross."

Anne could tell that the exchange was a familiar one for them. There was another thing she could tell. This was more than just a casual asking for the latest news from the jungle. It referred to something definite, something unmistakably vital.

Four

To Anne's dismay, it was the Rio Jara the *Lady Odyssey* pursued when they left the mission school that afternoon and not the more major Negro. There was less traffic along the Jara and the settlements were fewer and farther apart, the jungle growth even heavier along its banks. Civilization was growing more remote.

She worried about their new course. How in all this vastness of heat and forest and countless waterways could they ever expect to make contact with the rebels? In spite of Ross's assurances to her the other night about this being the *Lady Odyssey*'s regular run and the rebel force knowing it, she couldn't help the mounting tension of wondering and waiting.

She missed Ignacio and his cheerful chatter. She knew that Luiz missed the boy, as well. Ignacio had helped the deck hand with his chores. Anne decided to offer her own services. Hopefully, keeping active would take her mind off her concern with the voyage.

Her intention was to wash the day's dishes piled in the sink, but Luiz had something else in mind for her when she joined him in the galley and managed to communicate her desire to help. He had just brewed fresh coffee. He indicated the pot and a mug waiting on the counter, then pointed toward the bridge with his crooked, kindly smile.

Anne understood him. He wanted her to take coffee to Ross at the helm. She hesitated. After last night's disastrous encounter with Ross, she had promised herself to keep well out of his way. On the other hand, she experienced a longing to put Sister Veronica's affirmation to the test. *Was* she misjudging the man? Could she look at him closely again and this time find the sensitivity the nun claimed was hidden there under a tough shell?

Why such a discovery should matter at all to her was disturbing in itself, but Anne refused to examine it. She made her decision and poured the coffee.

Luiz nodded his approval. "*Café bom*, huh?"

She translated this to mean that Luiz thought his coffee was good. If you were a Brazilian, perhaps it was. But the stuff was so strong and thick that Anne had learned to pass it up and wondered how the two men could relish it. She smiled in polite agreement and headed forward with the mug.

If Ross was surprised to find her delivering his coffee instead of Luiz, he said nothing to indicate it when she joined him on the contained bridge. She tried to hand him the mug, but he kept his hands on the wheel and his eyes on the slowly unwinding river.

"Just set it over there, would you?" His voice was without a trace of impatience, which was a relief, since she never knew what mood she might find him in. He nodded toward a spot on his right atop the instrument console.

Anne had entered at his left, making his casual direction a small problem. She had never been in the wheelhouse before and hadn't realized how tight the space was. To reach across the front of him with the mug would interfere with his navigating. The only alternative was to squeeze behind him to the other side.

She hoped to slip by him with inches to spare but her hip brushed his backside as she stepped around him to the other side. There was no reason so brief and ordinary a contact should have affected her, but she experienced an instant jolt to her senses that left her shaken. Her trembling hand nearly spilled the coffee before she placed it safely next to a pair of rolled charts. This was ridiculous!

"Thank you," he said.

Her gaze went swiftly to his face, hoping he wasn't aware of her unsettled reaction. His eyes never left the river, but she could swear there was a glint of amusement in them. She even wondered if he had deliberately leaned back into her when she had passed behind him. She hadn't known him before to be capable of mischief, not of the humorous variety, but Sister Veronica maintained there were other levels to Ross McIntyre.

Anne searched his weathered face, trying to read him, to learn about the man Sister Veronica knew. What she sought was his character, and what she found was a jarring masculinity, a physical vitality that revealed mature features she hadn't noticed until now. There were attractive lines at the corners of his eyes, a sprinkling of gray in the thick, black hair at the nape of his bronzed neck, a firmness in the wide mouth that had a sensual—and lethal—quality about it.

This was a mistake! She had no business being here with him in this close, confined place.

"Something wrong?"

"No." He had felt her staring at him. She snatched at an excuse. "Yes. That grubby cap."

He reached up to tug at the skipper's cap crammed on the back of his head. "You don't like it?"

"It's a bit of an affectation, isn't it?"

"Hell, and I thought it was sexy."

She deserved his sarcasm this time. His cap was none of her business. For a change, though, he was smiling instead of scowling. "Your coffee is getting cold," she reminded him.

"Here, you take the wheel while I drink it."

"Me?"

"If Ignacio can handle it, you can."

She didn't want to steer the boat. She wanted to get out of here without risking another physical contact. Before she could object, he drew her to the helm, placed her hands on the wheel and stepped aside, leaving her in control. Anne didn't know whether her breathlessness was due to his touch or panic at feeling the surging power of the vessel suddenly under her hands.

"What do I do?" she pleaded.

"Just relax and hold it steady. All you have to do is stick to the main channel." He leaned against the console, drank his coffee and watched her with a lazy amusement.

"And how do I tell which is the main channel?"

"The darker water is the deeper, safe water. The lighter means shallows to avoid. You want to keep to where the current is running."

"Like that over there?" She nodded off toward the left where the water was roiling in a wedge shape.

"That's not current. That's disturbed water due to a snag or a sandbar. There's a lot of that in the dry season like this. Makes it tricky. Charts aren't much good, either. The river can change overnight. The only way to navigate it is by the seat of your pants."

"Look, you are definitely making me nervous." He didn't have to know his nearness in this rapidly shrinking wheelhouse was as much responsible for that as his vessel.

"You're doing okay," he assured her.

Ross went on drinking his coffee, watching her. He liked the way her slim hands gripped the wheel, the earnest little frown on her fine-boned face as she concentrated on the river. She was taking her responsibility very seriously, like a conscientious child would, and that delighted him.

Why did she keep on stirring these feelings deep inside him? A male arousal for that tempting woman's body was natural. But the urge to protect her confused and frustrated him. It was a need he didn't trust or want. He had experienced it before with another woman, and it had failed miserably. The residue of pain was always with him. Besides, Anne was no frail Claire. She was strong and independent. She didn't need any man's protection.

Then why did he go on admiring the honey-colored hair enriched by the light pouring into the wheelhouse, the teasing swell of her breasts? Why did he have these longings?

His gaze was scalding her. Anne couldn't go on dealing with the situation. They were approaching a bend in the river. It was an understandable reason for giving the wheel back to him.

"You'd better take over for this one," she said as matter-of-factly as she could. "Besides, I have a stack of dishes waiting for me in the galley."

She fled the wheelhouse, no more satisfied about the reality of Ross McIntyre than when she had arrived. She still didn't know just who or what he was, hadn't uncovered Sister Veronica's image of him. Only one thing was sharply evident. Being confined with him was inflammably dangerous to her equilibrium. But then she had known that from the beginning.

* * *

What was it?

Anne found herself sitting up in bed, clutching the sheet to her breasts and staring into the darkness of the cabin. The film of perspiration on her naked body was a result not of equatorial heat and humidity, but of nerves. She was actually shaking. Something had startled her out of a sound sleep in the middle of the night. Something fearful. A bad dream? If so, she didn't remember it.

Wanting the comfort of light, she groped for the switch on the lamp beside the bed. Before she could reach it, there was a wild cry from the jungle outside, a savage and mournful wail echoing through the night. This, then, was what had awakened her!

Heart racing, she turned on the lamp. The brightness dazzled her eyes. She went on gripping the sheet, straining to catch the sound of danger, her mind conjuring up memories of bloodthirsty jungle movies.

There was no noise now but the bugs popping against her window screen, trying to invade the cabin. Anne slowly calmed herself, trying to be reasonable. If there was anything to be alarmed about, she would be hearing Ross and Luiz moving around the boat, calling out to each other. But the *Lady Odyssey*, moored for the night in an inlet, was peacefully quiet.

Seconds later, the dismal yowling repeated itself and was answered by a similar scream deeper in the jungle. Some kind of animal on the prowl, Anne told herself firmly. A jaguar or an ocelot maybe. But it was enough to raise the hair on your neck. It certainly wasn't conducive to sleep.

Anne had no intention of shutting her eyes again, not until she had reassured herself that the boat wasn't under attack. Not bothering with undergarments, she slipped into cotton pants and a shirt and slid a pair of sandals on her feet. The soft night lamp burned comfortingly in the corridor as she left her cabin and made her way up the companionway.

There was a much brighter, unexpected light in the galley area. It came from the lamp suspended over the dining table. Apparently, she was not the only one aroused and unable to sleep.

Ross was sprawled there in one of the captain's chairs. His appearance shocked her. He looked both magnificent and terrible. Magnificent because he must have recently showered and his black hair was damp and appealingly tousled. Even from the doorway, she could smell the clean fragrance of the soap he had used. He, too, had dressed carelessly—his long feet bare, a fresh T-shirt hugging powerful shoulders and chest, a pair of tight jeans low on his hips. The jeans, faded and thin from countless launderings and obviously without any briefs under them, revealed the unmistakable bold outlines of his masculinity.

Anne would have retreated from so strong a temptation if there hadn't been the other terrible Ross to restrain her. There was despair in the slump of his shoulders, gauntness in the beard-shadowed face under the harshness of the overhead light and a tortured look in his weary eyes. His bleakness was more pronounced now than the night out on deck. She was seeing a man ravaged with grief and the sight was wrenching. She couldn't move. She could only stare at him with a deep sympathy that she knew instinctively he would resent.

He looked sick, and for a moment she suspected the worst because he was contemplating a bottle of whiskey on the table in front of him. But there was no glass and the bottle appeared unopened.

He felt her standing there and he looked up and met her worried gaze. His smile was slow and wry, his voice hoarse. "Don't worry. I'm not drunk. I haven't touched the stuff in almost two years. I don't know why I even keep it on board.

Yeah, I do. I keep it to remind myself that it isn't the answer, though there was a time when I tried like hell to prove that it was."

Anne was silent. What could she say when she had no idea what he was talking about?

"You couldn't sleep again, either, huh?" he asked.

She shook her head. "It wasn't the heat this time. I was asleep and then those awful shrieks woke me up."

Ross nodded understandingly. "Those are howler monkeys. Nothing to worry about. Must be a band of them nearby. They don't usually carry on like this until daybreak, but a big cat is probably worrying them."

"All that racket and it's just monkeys?"

"I know. The Indians say that the howlers can actually drive a man mad." He laughed grimly. "There are times when I almost believe that."

Anne went on standing there, feeling helpless. "Where—where is Luiz?"

"In his hammock. Luiz can sleep through anything." Ross's hands rubbed restlessly along the worn jeans stretched over his hard thighs. He seemed to be considering something. He nodded toward the chair across from him. "You play gin? Maybe we can play a few hands until the howlers decide to give up for the night."

Anne sensed it wasn't the monkeys that prevented him from sleeping. She hesitated, not wanting to intrude on his private pain. But he seemed so alone, and he must have wanted the company or he wouldn't have invited her.

She joined him silently at the table. He stretched up from the chair, reaching for a pack of playing cards on the shelf over his head. She watched his big hands rapidly shuffle the deck. There was a kind of desperation in the action, as if he were striving to thrust away an unwanted emotion.

He started to deal the cards when the terrifying roar of the howlers sounded again through the night. Anne stiffened, a shudder coursing through her. "I can't help it. They sound so—so human."

Ross, too, had turned rigid. His eyes were once more wearing the haunted look that tore at her insides. Voice deep and soft, he muttered a slow, anguished, "Like the cries of a lost soul."

Anne acted without thinking, her hand reaching across the table to cover his out of a deep, innate compassion. "What is it, Ross? What's wrong?"

She fully expected him to withdraw his hand, to curtly reject her desire to understand. He did neither. Instead, after a strained moment, he chuckled and asked a dry, "You got the rest of the night to listen?"

"Yes, if necessary," came her firm, unwavering response.

She could see his eyes widening in admiration over her solemn promise, and his reaction lit a glowing warmth inside her. She watched him, waiting for his decision.

When his hand did pull away, she thought with disappointment that he was refusing her offer. But it wasn't that. He brushed the cards aside on the table, then dragged both hands through his thick hair.

"Why not?" he said. "You might as well know what the rest of the Amazon territory knows. I lost something out there in the jungle, Anne. I lost something very precious. I keep on looking, and the whole river thinks I'm a damn fool because I won't give up. I *can't* give up."

"What did you lose, Ross?" she coaxed softly, knowing how important it was to exercise patience with him.

"My son," he confessed, a catch in his voice. "My little boy."

Anne was stunned. He had a child! He was a father! She didn't know why that should surprise her when he had already demonstrated how much he cared about kids. It was just that the Ross McIntyre she had been permitted to see didn't seem to belong in the family-man category. Until tonight, that is. All that Sister Veronica had been trying to tell her was now beginning to make sense.

"And his mother?" Anne asked uncertainly.

"Gone. Claire died when Danny disappeared."

"Were you—that is, was she your—"

"If you're asking was she my wife, the answer is yes. Almost five years. It wasn't a very strong marriage," he confided. "I was as much to blame for that as Claire, probably more. Hell, I was thirty-two when we met, and she was still in her early twenties. I was the one who was mature and should have had better sense. But nothing like her had ever come my way and I was dazzled. All I could see were those blue eyes and that red-gold hair. I would have done anything she asked. She was like that. People always wanted to do things for her. It was Claire's charm."

"You make her sound like—like a little girl."

Ross nodded. "In a way, she was. I don't mean she was spoiled, not in the usual mean way you think of. But having parents with money and who refused her nothing, she grew up never really dealing with reality. She couldn't see me for the roughneck lout I was, working on a construction project for her father in Florida. To Claire, I was this romantic, macho engineer building dreams all over the globe. But her father—" He shifted restlessly in his chair. "Well, he didn't want me for a son-in-law. And he was right. I didn't belong in their world."

"But you were married," Anne said.

"Because her folks couldn't deny her that, either."

"But you must have loved her if you married her."

Ross tossed his head with indecision. "I don't know anymore. Maybe. All I know is that by the time Danny came along, I wanted like crazy to make it work for us, even though by then the marriage started to have cracks in it. We'd begun to realize just how different we were."

Anne could hear the deep caring in his voice when he spoke of his son, and she realized the strong love he had for the boy and how hard the telling of this part of his story was for him.

"I wanted us to be a real family," Ross went on. "I didn't want Danny to have what I had growing up. No home, no mother and a vagabond of an old man hauling me all over the map. He'd dump me on relatives who didn't want me. Then he'd forget me and go off to work as a laborer at all these remote construction sites."

Hearing this explanation of his comfortless childhood, Anne was not surprised that Ross was so suspicious of any adult kindness or softness extended to him. The surprising thing was that under his tough cynicism was a vulnerability that expressed itself in a fierce love for a child, in a need to help those who couldn't help themselves.

"That's why I wouldn't settle for a separation when the Brazilian project came up," Ross continued. "They were building a new power plant in Manaus and they wanted me as one of the engineers. I couldn't turn it down because the money was so good. We had a lot of expenses. Claire liked nice things and I wouldn't let her folks pay for them. I shouldn't have dragged my family down here. I should have let Claire and Danny stay with her parents like her father wanted. But the job was a long one and I couldn't stand the thought of being away from my kid all those months."

Anne observed how the harsh line of his mouth softened whenever he referred to his son, and she could guess how much the boy had meant to him.

Ross was thoughtful for a moment, almost dreamy, while she waited patiently. Then he shrugged. "I don't know. Maybe I figured, too, that our marriage would work better down here away from the influence of her family and friends. Or maybe I was just being damned selfish. Also, there was the thing about the orchids."

Anne stared at him, puzzled. "Orchids?"

He nodded. "Yeah, Claire had this passion for orchids. She was always photographing them and collecting them, even belonged to some orchid society. That's why she was excited about coming to South America with me. She figured she could study orchids in the wild. She had a notion about doing a book. I didn't object. Hell, I was just grateful she and Danny would be with me."

Ross paused again. He could see in Anne's eyes that she realized he was struggling to go on. She recognized the massive effort it was costing him to deal with this portion of the story. Why, he wondered, did he feel it necessary to unburden himself to her, to pour out all his bitterness and anger and pain? He never talked about it to anyone, at least not in detail like this. So why her, a woman he had known for only a few days? Was it his low mood brought on by the howler monkeys that impelled him? Or did he sense an empathy and understanding in her that he badly needed? He wasn't sure. He only knew that he had to tell her, that somehow it mattered.

"I was glad when the work on the power plant started to wind down. It meant we could go home, even if Manaus had been perfectly safe and comfortable for us. But Claire was frustrated. Orchid-wise, Manaus had been a disappointment for her. So, when this business came up about a lumbering operation—"

"I don't understand," Anne murmured, hating to interrupt him when it was already so difficult for him.

"Yeah. Well, the Brazilian government was considering placing a lumber mill right up here along the Jara. Nothing ever came of it, but they wanted a feasibility study and they needed engineering input. I was asked to join the team they put together. When Claire heard they were promising to send us up here on a fully-equipped, modern ship and that, as an incentive, wives and kids were welcome to come along, she jumped at it. Her chance to see orchids in the wild. I wasn't happy about it, bringing them right up into the jungle like that. But the people in charge promised it was okay. Nothing to worry about. Done all the time. Besides . . ."

"The little girl, again, you couldn't refuse," Anne said.

"Something like that, I suppose." A muscle in his jaw began to twitch and he rushed his words now in a tight, clipped voice, needing to hurry through the tragic episode. "Claire wasn't supposed to go into the jungle on her own. She was supposed to accompany the guided tours that had been arranged for the families. But some local rubber gatherer told her about this rare orchid he knew of. It was out in the bush where the tours weren't going. He promised to take her there when he went to collect his latex. Claire didn't ask me. She knew what my answer would be."

Ross's voice turned raspy with taut emotion. "She never planned to take Danny along. One of the local girls was meant to watch him while she was gone. But the girl didn't turn up. Claire couldn't stand the thought of not going, of not having her damn way. I didn't know anything about it. I was with the crew at the mill site. I didn't know she went off in that dugout with her camera and Danny. I didn't know her guide left her there in the jungle with the orchids and Danny while he went away to harvest his trees."

Ross pushed away from the table, his voice suddenly flat, as though it could no longer support his desolation. "Claire was dead by the time her guide came back for her. We figured she must have climbed into one of the trees to get a better shot at the flowers. There were marks on her arm. Snake bite. It wasn't the venom that killed her, though. When the snake struck, she probably lost her balance, fell out of the tree. They said her neck was broken."

"And Danny?" Anne whispered, her heart heavy at the unbearable thought of the small, helpless boy alone there in the jungle with his dead mother.

Ross shook his head, his chest heaving as he expelled a long, tired sigh. "No sign of him, not a trace. We didn't know whether he wandered back to the river when he couldn't rouse his mother or—or what. We searched. I remember how we searched. I don't remember the part after that. I don't remember how I was when they finally gave up looking, when they made me give up. They said I went all crazy and wild, that I actually had to be restrained when the ship took us back to Manaus. But I don't remember it."

Through a haze of tears, Anne watched Ross come to his feet. He began to pace around the cramped space of the dinette and the adjoining galley, his hands absently touching utensils on the counter, items on the open shelf above the table.

"Those weeks in Manaus were pure hell," he said. "I drank. I drank a lot. Then I realized how stupid I was being, that booze was nothing but self-pity. That's when I decided what to do. I took my savings and bought the *Lady Odyssey*. I figured I could run the rivers as a trader. That way I would make a living and be able to hear all the news from the bush. I never gave up hoping that one day somebody out there would know about Danny and tell me."

"How long, Ross? How long has it been?"

"Two years. The experts down here think I'm nuts. They tell me that no young child could possibly survive in the jungle on his own. They say people disappear out there all the time and are never heard of again. They think I should just accept that and give up. But every time I look into the jungle, I wonder if he could be anywhere near, and every time I ask someone for news from the bush I hope . . . well, you know."

"And—and in all this time, you never once considered going back home to the States?"

He stopped pacing and faced her, his voice raw with desperation. "How could I? Not without *knowing*. If he is still alive—and I won't let myself believe that he isn't somehow—then I have to be here for him. You understand?"

Anne did understand. She saw him hurting, his eyes hollow with misery, and she shared his heartbreaking torment. She longed to reach out to him, to ease his pain, but she didn't know whether he would accept her comfort. She had never felt so helpless. All she could do was listen.

"Two years," he said, his voice breaking. "And he was so little. So damned little. He's going on six now. He's probably forgotten me. I don't know why I should mind that so much, but I do."

"Ross—"

He didn't hear her. His face contorted as his fist came slamming against the bulkhead between the lounge and galley with all the rage and frustration that had been festering within him for two years. "It shouldn't have happened! I shouldn't have let it happen! I tried to tell myself it was Claire's fault, but he truth is I'm to blame!"

"No," Anne said. "How could it be your fault? You didn't even know they went off like that."

"I'm to blame," he insisted. "I'm at fault for bringing them to South America in the first place. For letting Claire talk me into taking them upriver when I knew better. They'd be safe today if it weren't for me."

Anne couldn't stand this anymore. She couldn't go on sitting here watching him lacerate himself, listening to the self-anger that was tearing him apart. She had to to go him.

Leaving the chair, she crossed the dinette and stood close in front of him. "Ross, you can't go on punishing yourself like this. You did everything a husband and father is supposed to do."

His dark, aching eyes met hers. "But I didn't protect them!" he cried hoarsely. "A man is supposed to protect his family, and I didn't protect them!"

It was no use. Words weren't going to console his anguish. Anne could think of only one thing to do. It seemed like the most natural action in the world when her arms reached out and went around him. For a few brief seconds, he stiffened in resistance. Then she felt him melting against her, welcoming her embrace. And something that was deep and terrible and infinitely cruel suddenly released itself as his broad shoulders convulsed with his dry sobs. Anne's eyes were not dry. Tears of sympathy and relief over his outpouring welled as she went on hugging him, her hands stroking his hard back, slowly soothing him.

They clung like that for long moments and she wasn't sure just when the mood of their closeness altered. She only knew that, at some inevitable point, she was not holding him anymore. He was holding her. Holding her tightly, ferociously, with a swelling need that went far beyond comforting or gratitude.

Anne lifted her head from where it had been tucked under his chin, nestled against the solid warmth of his shoulder. Her gaze sought his with both desire and uncertainty. His eyes, as deep and green as the jungle outside, probed her gaze silently. There was a sultriness in his dilated pupils, like the hot, humid night.

"Ross?" she whispered.

"I know," he muttered thickly. "I know."

She could feel his breath mingling with hers as his parted mouth lowered and angled across hers—possessing her, branding her with his lips. All the steamy wildness of the torrid rain forest went into that kiss.

Anne was immersed in an overflow of sensations: the stubble on his jaw rubbing her like dark sandpaper; the primitive, masculine taste of him; his wet tongue invading her mouth, curling dominantly around her tongue.

She had never known it was possible to experience such a blast of raw sexuality as she clutched at him fiercely, answering his need with her own need. Her tongue mated with his, her moans echoed his guttural moans.

She was greedy. She wanted more of him. She wanted to touch him intimately. Her fingers clawed at his T-shirt, releasing it from his jeans. Then without inhibition, her hands slid under the shirt, searching the slick contours of his sweat-dampened skin. She roamed the expanse of his solid flesh, familiarizing herself with the sleek strength of his back, his ribs, the slabs of rock-hard muscle above his ribs. Her hands buried themselves in the thick mat of black hair furring his chest. She hadn't realized a man's body could be so exciting, so completely arousing. His eyes were closed in a mind-drugging passion, his breathing harsh as her fingers teased his flat nipples to a pebble-hard erectness.

Ross wasn't kissing her now. His hands had slipped inside the waistband of her cotton pants. Realizing she was wearing no undergarment, he found the contact of his fingers against her naked flesh electrifying. Hands cupping her cheeks, he dragged her with him as he sagged weakly against the bulkhead behind him. Clamped between his parted legs as she was, Anne was made fully aware of the awesome swelling she had provoked.

He wanted more than just her awareness. Freeing one of his hands from her bottom, he went under his T-shirt and caught her by a wrist. His fingers guided her down and under the tight waistband of his jeans. The pressure of her hand, together with his, forced the snap, parting the zipper by several inches. Her fingers, brushing crisp hairs, squeezed lower under his direction until her trapped hand was suddenly seared by the tip of his tumescence, silk over steel. Her fingers fluttered, unintentionally teasing his confined hardness. Groaning, he squirmed and thrust against her. His face was flushed, his breathing heavy. That she could create so powerful a response in a strong man both amazed and

touched Anne. She had never really experienced this won-
drous revelation before. Not with Dane, not with any man.

As if her realization communicated itself to Ross, jarring
his memory, his eyes flew open. The green fire in them had
abruptly died to cold ashes. He stared at her, his voice gritty
with accusation. "What in sweet hell are we doing?"

Stung, Anne's hands pulled away from him. "What is
it?" she pleaded. "What's wrong?"

He straightened, fastening his jeans, pulling his T-shirt
down over the waistband. "I'll tell you what's wrong. Another two minutes and I would have taken you right here on
the floor."

"Would that have been so awful?" Anne demanded, able
to admit to herself now how much she wanted him. And this
time she had been willing to do something about it because
she knew he wanted her with the same intense need.

"Under the circumstances, it would have been a mistake."

"What circumstances?"

"You forgetting that guy upriver you're so anxious to
free?"

She was stricken by his reference to Dane, by the meaning behind words as obvious and cruel as a slap. Damn him!
Did he think she was some kind of wanton? That she in-
dulged carelessly in relationships whenever the mood
prompted her?

"For your information," Anne told him, voice low and
steady, though she was quivering inside, "I'm not in the
habit of wanting two men at the same time. My feelings for
my ex-husband have to do with conscience and nothing
else."

However controlled she sounded, he must have read the
hurt and bewilderment. He started to reach out to her.
"Anne—"

She stepped away from him before he could touch her. "The howler monkeys seem to have quit for the night. I think I'll do the same."

She didn't look at him. She couldn't. She turned away and headed for her cabin. She felt exhausted suddenly, all squeezed out. And confused. Why, even now, after all the emotional intimacy they had just shared, did Ross persist in thinking the worst of her? And when—*when* were the rebels going to make contact with them so that she could put this unendurable turmoil behind her?

Five

The grunting sow lifted its wet snout and glared at Ross out of a pair of small, mean-tempered eyes. The animal seemed to be taking his measure, maybe wondering which one of them was in the nastier mood this morning. If it came to a showdown over the subject, Ross figured the pig stood a good chance of winning the contest. He was in a bad state after last night's encounter with Anne, but the sow seemed angrier.

She probably has reason to be, he thought as he stood on the dock and contemplated the creature in its bamboo cage. He had watched while a half dozen men in the village cornered the pig, captured her and squeezed her into the cage. She had been happy about none of it.

Those half dozen men were gathered around him now on the dock where the cage had been situated, waiting for his decision with grave expressions on their faces. The rest of the villagers, watching from the riverbank, were wearing those same matter-of-life-or-death looks.

Luiz, at Ross's side, had more tension on his battered face than the others. It was understandable since his honor was at stake in this transaction. The village was no ordinary village, and the pig was no ordinary pig. It was Luiz's home village and his cousins were sending the sow upriver as a wedding present to relatives in the next village. The transporting of the animal was an important undertaking, and if Senhor Ross refused to carry the sow on the *Lady Odyssey*...

Ross didn't like it. Luiz knew he never took livestock on his boat. The *Lady Odyssey* looked disreputable enough without having pigs squealing on her decks. Besides, Brazilian pigs, often crossed with wild hogs from the forest, could be wicked things. He wasn't convinced the bamboo bars of the cage were stout enough to contain the animal, though half the village had assured him the sow couldn't possibly escape.

Ross sighed, knowing it wasn't the pig provoking his sour mood, but his memories of last night. His loins were still aching for what his body craved but what his conscience denied. He thought too much of Anne now to want to hurt her.

Heck, face it, he thought about her all the time. He thought about the way she was, the way he had refused to see her until the central substance of her being had demanded his recognition of her as a strong, mature, capable woman. Nothing at all like Claire. Anne was someone to admire and respect, someone with depth. He was constantly discovering new facets to her that intrigued and pleased him.

He thought about her a lot, all right. Mostly he thought about having her in his bed, of her lush body going all wild and wanton under his. So much for his lofty admiration of her.

Well, it wasn't going to happen. He wasn't going to take her to bed, even though she had made it pretty clear last night that she was perfectly willing. Where would it get them? Neither one of them was the type to involve themselves in some quick affair and then extricate themselves without pain. And it couldn't be any more than a passing affair when her whole future was waiting for her back in New Orleans. And his future? Well, that was the whole point. He didn't have one. He had nothing to offer but his crummy boat and his endless waiting . . . and all his torment over Danny. No woman deserved that.

Anyway, there was still the ex-husband. Whatever Anne's denial last night, Ross wasn't convinced that she didn't have strong feelings for the man—maybe feelings she didn't know she kept or couldn't admit to herself. Why else would she be enduring every hell to reach him?

Maybe he was all wrong about the ex. Maybe he was just plain jealous. But he still wasn't going to risk either her suffering or his own. Both of them had too much to deal with to go and further complicate the situation with an intimate relationship that stood a snowball's chance in hell of surviving.

He wished his body would start listening to the wisdom his mind was ready to obey. He couldn't stop wanting her, couldn't shake those lustful images of how she had been last night when he had held her—the fantastic heat and softness of her breasts crushed against his chest, her woman's scent, the warm, wet, inviting cavern of her mouth, her hands inside his shirt and jeans touching him like that. His thoughts were driving him nuts.

He also couldn't shake his remorse over the insensitive way he had resisted her. Damn, how could he have humiliated her like that after all her honest compassion?

"Senhor Ross?" Luiz, growing impatient, was waiting for his decision about the pig.

Ross knew he couldn't disappoint Luiz or his village. He answered him in Portuguese with a reluctant, "All right, Luiz, we deliver the wedding gift."

Luiz grinned, the men on the dock shouted and the rest of the villagers on the riverbank congratulated each other. The sow was less ecstatic as her cage was hoisted and borne toward the boat.

Ross, directing the operation, caught sight of Anne standing at the deck rail watching the proceedings. Their eyes met and he tried to tell her with his gaze what he had been unable to tell her with his tongue: *Whatever else happened last night, thank you for being there when it mattered. For listening. For caring.*

He didn't know if she understood. She had already lowered her gaze. If she was rejecting his message, it was no more than he deserved. But God help him, it hurt.

Anne couldn't trust herself to look at him anymore. The mere sight of him rocked her senses to a treacherous degree. He was down on the dock. She was up here at the rail. It should have been safe. But even with this separation, with no more than a glance, she was able to notice things about him that fed her lightheaded longing and had her swallowing nervously.

His faded blue work shirt had come unbuttoned just above the waistband of his jeans. The gap disclosed a seductive glimpse of the indentation that was his navel, shadowed by whorls of dark, curling hair. Higher, in the V formed by the open collar of the shirt, the hair was more generous. Tiny beads of perspiration had collected here, clinging to the hairs. It made her remember last night, what it had felt like to touch him there. Made her wonder what his skin would taste like in those places. Faintly salty, distinctly male?

Last night. Sweet heaven, she couldn't get her mind off last night. She couldn't stop thinking how arousing their encounter had been. Was a woman supposed to want a man with this kind of forceful intensity?

Ross wanted her, too. She wasn't wrong about that. She had clearly felt his desire last night, could feel it still this morning. But he would do nothing about it, would permit her to do nothing. She knew him so well now, and yet she didn't know him at all. She didn't understand his resistance.

Dane? No, there was much more to it than the subject of her ex-husband. She could sense that Dane had merely been his half-believed excuse.

But Ross was right, Anne realized as she turned away from the rail. Their wants had to be resisted. She had to stop thinking about her longings. She had to concentrate on her mission, remember what poor Dane must be suffering as he waited for her to reach him. Not just for Dane's sake but for her own, as well. Because it wasn't just her body anymore that was trying to betray her. It was her heart, too. And something told her that to trust her heart to Ross McIntyre would be opening a door to disaster. Maybe this explained his resistance. Wise Ross. She could be equally wise. No, *must* be equally wise.

Praying that the rebel contact would occur soon, that she could free herself from this highly-charged situation, Anne spent the long morning hiding out on the stern deck where, curled in a deck chair, she watched the river stretch away behind the rumbling *Lady Odyssey*. Her only company was the pig, whose cage had been parked nearby under the canopy to keep her out of the sun. Not exactly the companion Anne would have chosen since the odor that came from the cage was anything but pleasant. She could have settled herself on the open forward deck but, like the pig, that would have meant suffering the broiling sun. It also would have meant enduring Ross's gaze from his position in the wheelhouse. It was safer to stay with the pig.

Ross came nowhere near the stern, avoiding Anne as she was avoiding him. Even at lunch they didn't meet. Luiz took a tray to him on the bridge. Who are we kidding? Anne wondered. But after grabbing a boiled egg and a slice of watermelon, she fled back to her refuge on the stern deck.

There was no question of staying inside. The air was oppressive enough outdoors. In the cabins, it was impossible. Luiz, coming around to check on the sow, informed Anne with gestures that it was going to rain. Anne could believe it. She hadn't felt the air this miserably heavy or sticky since the voyage began.

The pig, too, must have sensed a change in the atmosphere. She grew restive in her pen. Anne, reading glasses in place and trying without much success to concentrate on the pharmaceutical report in her lap, made an effort to ignore the animal.

By midafternoon, this was no longer possible. Thick clouds were massing in the sky and the sow was stirring around her cage and complaining noisily. Anne put her reading glasses and work folder away and regarded the creature through eyes burning from lack of sleep. She was sympathetic but had no idea how to go about calming an unhappy pig. Besides, she didn't like the way the animal was looking at her, as if it were all her fault.

The channel was wide here, and when the wind behind the rain clouds rushed in over the jungle seconds later, swaying the treetops against the shore, the river suddenly came alive with small, dancing waves. The yacht began to rock. Nothing that was threatening. Except to the pig. She went wild in her cage. The hard, powerful snout began ramming the bars.

Anne came to her feet in alarm as she heard the bamboo cracking under the battering force of the animal determined to escape her prison. "Hey, don't do that!" she cried, and thought instantly how absurd her command was. Fetching one of the men would be more useful.

Anne turned and raced toward the bow. She met Luiz halfway along the narrow side deck. "Trouble, Luiz! The pig is getting out!"

The deck hand may not have followed her English, but he did understand her panic. He sped with her back to the stern where the sow was making remarkable progress in destroying its cage.

Luiz's solution to the dilemma was to fling his skinny body across the cage, arms and legs embracing the bamboo bars in a questionable struggle to prevent the collapse of the pen. His helpless eyes sought Anne's. "Senhor Ross!" he shouted. *"Apressar! Apressar!"*

He wanted Ross. Fast. Leaving Luiz draped across the cage like a desperate spider, Anne flew toward the bow. When she burst into the wheelhouse, flushed and breathless, Ross turned from the helm to stare at her in amazement.

"Luiz needs you!" she gasped. "It's the pig! She's breaking out of her cage!"

The air was hot, but Ross made it even hotter, blistering her ears with his explicit curses. "I knew that sow meant trouble when we brought her on board! Here, take over the wheel!"

"A-are you crazy? You can't leave me up here on m-my own to steer the boat while you—"

"Anne, it's an emergency. You have to. I can't anchor the boat out here in this current. Just stick to the main channel like I taught you. I'll be back before you miss me."

He put her hands on the wheel and was out the door and gone while she was still stammering her objections. She found herself suddenly in charge of the helm and hating it.

The *Lady Odyssey* apparently didn't care for the fact that she was at the controls, either. The old yacht began to buck in the choppy waters. Anne fought to keep the vessel on its path while eyeing a sky threatening to discharge a torrent of rain at any second.

Where was Ross? Where was Luiz? What was happening with the pig? Two of her questions were answered a moment later when the pig, who had achieved her freedom after all, came charging across the foredeck below with Luiz in close pursuit. Anne watched in astonishment as they passed out of her line of vision and around the other side of the boat. She had no idea where Ross had gotten to.

Seconds later, Luiz and the pig were back in view. This time the chase was reversed. Now the maddened sow was after a very frightened Luiz. Ross had finally appeared with a rope and began yelling at Luiz. Anne figured out that he wanted the deck hand to drive the pig his way so that he could lasso the animal.

It's a screwball comedy, Anne thought. Only it wasn't very funny. Not with her alone here at the wheel worried about a bouncing boat. Not with the rain that was suddenly coming in sheets, lashing the windows of the bridge, obscuring her view of the river.

She didn't know how to turn on the window wipers; she didn't know which one of the many buttons and knobs on the instrument panel worked them. And she couldn't see the river clearly. She bobbed her head, peered through the rain-washed glass, swore at her frustration, but she couldn't properly see. Was that disturbed water looming ahead? A sign of a snag or sandbar? Or just wind-driven waves on the channel. Which? *Which?*

Somewhere in her line of vision, another image registered itself. It was the sight of Ross, drenched by the downpour and wrestling with the pig on the foredeck. Luiz was dancing around them, trying to wrap the rope around the enraged sow. Suddenly Ross glanced up from the tussle, spotting the trouble on the river ahead, confirming what Anne had been about to determine.

"Starboard!" he shouted while still struggling with the pig. "Bring her over to starboard! *Now! Fast!*"

Starboard, starboard, Anne thought frantically. To the left? Yes, she was sure *starboard* meant to the left. Would that do it? Leave them in the clear? If only she could see. She swung the wheel, aiming the vessel to the left.

The images came very rapidly then, too quickly for Anne to believe them: the sandbar fast approaching; Ross and Luiz and the pig going down on the deck in a tangle of arms and legs and wild curses; the *Lady Odyssey* plowing head-on into the sandbar with all the impact of a runaway train hurtling itself into a mountainside.

A long shudder passed simultaneously through Anne and the vessel. And then there was stillness. But not silence. Someone was bellowing at her. Bellowing at her angrily. Collecting her senses, she realized that Ross was clinging like a fly to the exterior of the wheelhouse. His long arm shot through the open side window, groped for a switch and killed the engine. His eyes were blazing with fury.

"You've hung us up on a sandbar! I hollered at you to turn starboard! We would have cleared her if you'd turned starboard! Didn't you hear me?"

As always when under a heated verbal attack, Anne's arms wound around her middle, hugging herself protectively. "I heard you."

"Then why in the name of all that's holy did you bring her over to port?"

"I thought starboard meant to the left, that's why. And stop shouting at me!"

He went right on shouting. "Of all the idiotic things! Not to know starboard from port! Everybody knows what starboard and port mean!"

"Well, I don't! Ask me the composition of aspirin and I'll come up with a reasonable answer! But I don't pretend to know nautical terms! I'm no sailor! And, anyway, why didn't you just point to the direction you meant?"

"Because both my hands were busy, that's why! I don't believe this!"

"That makes two of us! I don't believe you'd hand the wheel over to me like that, leave me all alone up here in a confusing situation and then have the gall to blame me when—when— And another thing! Why do people with boats go around yelling *starboard* and *port*? Why can't they use plain left and right? Why— Ross?"

She had just realized that Ross's face was no longer hanging at the window. Somewhere during her angry outpouring, it had sunk from sight. Anne rushed to the window, peering down.

Ross was huddled on the deck below, legs drawn up to his chest, head buried against his knees, body shaking with convulsions. He must have lost his hold on the wet wall of the wheelhouse, dropped to the deck, injured himself.

Fear swept over Anne. She forgot her anger, forgot everything but a reckless need to reach him. Rushing through the door, she descended from the wheelhouse, raced across the deck and knelt at the side of his crouching figure. His body was still shaking and strange, muffled noises were coming from his face hidden against his upraised knees.

Heart slamming like a jackhammer, Anne put a hand on his shoulder, her voice hoarse with worry. "Ross, what is it? Have you—I'll never forgive myself if I—Ross?"

His head came up from his knees. Spikes of wet hair were plastered to his brow, dirt streaked one cheek. And he was laughing. Laughing like a devil.

Anne stared at him in amazement. "You're not hurt! I thought you— Damn it, it isn't funny!" She swiped at his shoulder still quaking with mirth.

"Yeah, it is," he choked. "It suddenly struck me how really funny the whole thing is."

She went on staring at him. This was a Ross she hadn't experienced before, one capable of boyish hilarity. Her discovery both confused and delighted her.

He rubbed the back of his hand across his eyes and shook his head. "You know," he confessed, "I think that's the first time I've laughed—really laughed—in over two years. I've forgotten how good it feels."

His gaze, suddenly sober, met hers. Anne realized that her heart was still racing, but with a different emotion now. She read gratitude in his eyes. He was actually thanking her for his laughter.

The moment, pleasurable though it was, threatened to be unsafe. She swallowed, then forced herself to sound ordinary, impersonal. "It's stopped raining. We even have the sun again."

"Yeah. Well, that's the tropics for you. Everything is sudden."

Yes, Anne thought. Especially emotions. He was still looking at her in that throat-tightening way. She fought for self-control. "Where—where are Luiz and the pig?"

Ross looked around. "Damned if I know. When we hit the sandbar, I let the pig go. All I could think of was leaping for the wheelhouse and your throat. Fine time to ask, but are you okay?"

"I'm all right. The collision wasn't as bad as it seemed."

He heaved himself to his feet, brushing at his wet jeans. By the time Anne stood beside him, Luiz had appeared from the direction of the stern, looking decidedly mournful.

Ross questioned him, then turned to Anne. "Looks like we've proved one thing today. Pigs can swim."

"She got away?"

"Clean away. Last Luiz saw of her, she was overboard and heading for the shore. No pork for the wedding feast."

"Oh, Ross, I'm so sorry. And your boat—what have I done to your boat?"

He smiled at her, a patient, tolerant Ross she couldn't believe. "Easy. We'll see."

He and Luiz went to the bow rail and looked down. There was a long silence, and then Luiz wailed an unhappy, hand-wringing, "Aye-yi-yi."

Anxious, Anne joined the man. "What is it? Holes? Are we going to sink?"

"Nothing so awful," Ross reassured her. "It's all soft sand and mud, no rocks. But, Ms. Richmond, when you run a boat aground, you don't fool around. Looks like we're caught good and tight on this thing."

"Can we get off?"

"Time to find out. Hey, don't look like that. We're going to be okay, and we haven't lost anyone but the pig."

Anne tried to share his confidence, waiting for the men as they went below deck to check the forward bilge for damage or leaks. They reported that everything was sound, but Ross was not satisfied until he went over the side, inspecting both the hull and their situation from the muck of the sandbar.

He's an engineer, Anne thought. He'll know how to get us off.

But Ross's knowledge, along with the powerful reverse thrust of the *Lady Odyssey*'s engine minutes later, was not enough to free them.

The two men conferred, and then Ross explained his decision to her. "We're stuck here without help. The next village isn't too far upriver. I'm sending Luiz there in the outboard to round up his cousins."

"What can they do?"

"Not much in their dugouts, but I'm hoping with enough shovels and tow lines we'll be able to dig under and ease her off. Besides," he said with a grin, "I'm too much of a coward to face them until Luiz has gone ahead and softened the blow about the pig."

Anne, watching the outboard lowered from its davits, prayed that Luiz's kin would agree to return with him. She hated to think what would happen if they didn't. More delays, more waiting. Would this voyage with all its heartaches never end?

When the deck hand disappeared around a bend in the river, Ross went off to his cabin to shower and change. Anne returned to her deck chair in the stern. She didn't expect to fall asleep, but after last night's wakefulness, after too many tensions, both physical and emotional, she was exhausted. She drifted off in the deck chair and slept as though drugged.

She came awake to the savory odor of vegetable soup.

Anne stirred and sat up, her nose wrinkling in puzzlement. She leaned forward in the chair and widened her eyes in surprise. Ross was seated opposite her. He had placed a small table between them. A tray laden with bowls of steaming soup and chunks of the local cassava bread acquired at their last stop had been perched temptingly on the table.

"Supper," he announced.

"Supper? Have I been asleep that long? What time is it?"

He didn't need to answer her she realized, glancing toward the flaming sky over the river. The red disk of the sun was settling into the jungle.

"Thought we'd picnic on the deck," he explained. "The air is a little more bearable out here."

Not by much, Anne realized, fanning herself with one of the napkins he had provided on the tray. Instead of cooling the air, the rain had only made it muggier. "Is it always like this?" she wondered out loud.

"Only two temperatures in the Amazon, Anne. Hot and hotter. Fact is, the *Lady Odyssey* is equipped with air conditioning. It wasn't working, though, when I got her, and I never repaired it. Too expensive to run and Luiz and I never minded the heat."

Luiz, Anne suddenly remembered. "Luiz isn't back yet?"

"Not yet."

"But he left hours ago."

"Don't worry. He'll get here. Aren't you hungry?"

"Starving."

"Then eat. It's only canned soup," he apologized. "I'm not much of a hand in the galley."

Anne didn't object. The vegetable soup was thick and appetizing, and though the unfamiliar cassava bread was on the bland side, it was filling. Besides, there was something endearing in the way he'd proudly prepared the meal then carried it out to her. They ate in silence, enjoying the tropic sunset.

She had emptied her bowl and was placing it on the tray when it occurred to her that there was no lingering twilight in the tropics. It would soon be dark. "If Luiz does get here with the men," she said, "they won't be able to work without light."

Ross didn't answer her for a moment. Then he set his own bowl on the tray and said, "Luiz won't be back before morning, Anne. Things don't work with that kind of speed down here. He'll be up half the night bargaining with his cousins before they strike a deal. We'll be lucky if they get around to us by noon tomorrow, but they will come."

She stared at him. He had known all along that Luiz wouldn't return tonight and had avoided telling her. Why? And then she understood. They were alone here together, just the two of them. There was the long night ahead with no one but themselves.

She knew what the situation offered, and he knew it, too. It was there in his face, in his pulse beating in the hollow of his tanned throat, in his strong hands clenching the arms of his chair. She had never been so totally aware of him. Or of her longing.

The point of her tongue passed over lips that were suddenly dry. Her voice was husky when she spoke, huskier than it had ever been before. "Ross?"

All the need and yearning that had been swelling inside her since last night went into that single word. She no longer cared about restraint. He understood her. Further expression wasn't necessary. Not when they had been communicating their mounting desires for each other in a score of ways since the voyage began.

The sight of her tongue slowly licking her lips aroused him. Ross knew that her action was not intentional, not meant to be seductive, but his insides went warm and liquid watching it happen. She would never know what it cost him when his hands tightened with determination on the chair arms, when in a voice rigid and rough he told her, "No, Anne, it can't happen."

That isn't what he's saying, she thought. He's really saying *No, Anne, I won't let it happen.* She understood that much, all right. She even understood that Ross was no ordinary man, that lovemaking had to bear a form of commitment for him. She couldn't have been so susceptible to him otherwise. What she failed to understand was why he was unable to offer that commitment, the emotional caring that transcended the physical. That's all she asked of him, and he must realize that.

She couldn't take this tension anymore, this lack of verbal communication. This time she wouldn't let him avoid an explanation.

The more
you love romance . . .
the more
you'll love this offer

Mail this
heart today!
(See inside)

**Join us on a Silhouette® Honeymoon
and we'll give you
4 free books
A free Victorian picture frame
And a free mystery gift**

IT'S A
SILHOUETTE HONEYMOON—
A SWEETHEART OF A FREE OFFER!
HERE'S WHAT YOU GET:

1. Four New Silhouette Desire® Novels—FREE!

Take a Silhouette Honeymoon with your four exciting romances—yours
FREE from Silhouette Reader Service™. Each of these hot-off-the-press
novels brings you the passion and tenderness of today's greatest love
stories . . . your free passports to bright new worlds of love and foreign
adventure.

2. Lovely Victorian Picture Frame—FREE!

This lovely Victorian pewter-finish miniature is
perfect for displaying a treasured photograph. And
it's yours FREE as added thanks for giving our
Reader Service a try!

3. An Exciting Mystery Bonus—FREE!

You'll be thrilled with this surprise gift. It is useful as well as practical.

4. Free Home Delivery!

Join the Silhouette Reader Service™ and enjoy the convenience of pre-
viewing 6 new books every month delivered right to your home. Each
book is yours for only $2.24* each—a saving of 26¢ off the cover price.
And there is no extra charge for postage and handling. It's a sweetheart
of a deal for you! If you're not completely satisfied, you may cancel at
anytime, for any reason, simply by sending us a note or shipping statement marked "cancel" or by returning any shipment to us at our cost.

5. Free Insiders' Newsletter!

You'll get our monthly newsletter, packed with news about your favorite
writers, upcoming books, even recipes from your favorite authors.

6. More Surprise Gifts!

Because our home subscribers are our most valued readers, when you
join the Silhouette Reader Service™, we'll be sending you additional free
gifts from time to time—as a token of our appreciation.

START YOUR SILHOUETTE HONEYMOON TODAY—JUST COM-
PLETE, DETACH AND MAIL YOUR FREE-OFFER CARD

*Terms and prices subject to change without notice. Sales tax applicable in NY.

Get your fabulous gifts
ABSOLUTELY FREE!

MAIL THIS CARD TODAY.

PLACE
HEART STICKER
HERE

GIVE YOUR HEART TO SILHOUETTE

Yes! Please send me my four Silhouette Desire® novels FREE, along with my free Victorian picture frame and free mystery gift. I wish to receive all the benefits of the Silhouette Reader Service™ as explained on the opposite page.

NAME _____
(PLEASE PRINT)

ADDRESS _____ APT. _____

CITY _____ STATE _____

ZIP CODE _____

225 CIS ACEU
(U-SIL-D-01/91)

SILHOUETTE READER SERVICE™ "NO-RISK" GUARANTEE

—There's no obligation to buy—and the free gifts remain yours to keep.

—You pay the low subscribers'-only price and receive books before they appear in stores.

—You may end your subscription anytime by sending us a note or shipping statement marked "cancel" or by returning any shipment to us at our cost.

START YOUR
SILHOUETTE HONEYMOON TODAY.
JUST COMPLETE, DETACH AND MAIL YOUR
FREE-OFFER CARD.

"Is it Dane?" she demanded hoarsely. "Do you still see my ex-husband as some kind of rival? Because if that is what this is all about, I promise you that Dane no longer means anything to me. Not in that way, Ross. It's complicated, the reason I'm helping him, but I can try—"

"No," he said gruffly. "You don't have time to tell me. Okay, I admit I was—well, jealous, even when I had no right to be. But I know better now."

She leaned forward in her chair, her posture as insistent as her voice. "Then what is it?"

His fingers dug into the chair arms, fighting her, fighting his craving for her. "I don't want you to want me, Anne. And I don't want me to want you."

"Why? *Why?*"

"Isn't that obvious? Because it's no good. Because you're not the kind of woman to get involved and then walk away without getting hurt. And you would be hurt. *I* would be hurt. Look at us, Anne. We're about three universes apart. You're French wine and a night at the opera. Well, I drink beer, and for me *A Night at the Opera* means the Marx Brothers."

"You're wrong. Okay, I don't care for beer. But I also don't care for opera, and I love the Marx Brothers. Don't categorize me, Ross. I'm not the elegant society creature you think I am. If anything, I'm jeans and popcorn in front of the fire after a tough work day. And this is silly. This isn't what your resistance is all about."

"Isn't it? Aren't you forgetting I made that mistake once before in my life and how I paid for it?"

Claire, she realized. But there was more to it than that, much more. "I don't believe you," she persisted. "It isn't just life-styles we're talking about here. That's too easy."

"Anne, listen to me. I can't be what you need. I don't have it to offer. Not anymore. The part of me that isn't hollow inside is all chewed up. You saw that last night, and you know why. No woman deserves a man like that, and I'm not going to see you risk the pain.''

Oh, he was so wrong, so frustratingly wrong! He didn't know at all what he was. But she did. Bit by bit, layer by layer, she had uncovered the genuine Ross McIntyre under his tough, defensive armor. She knew the man he was, the man Sister Veronica had tried to tell her about. The caring, sensitive, gentle Ross. He couldn't hide from her anymore, but he was hiding from himself.

Anne tried to reach him, to make him see just who he was. "All right, you're hurting, and it's understandable. But, Ross, that doesn't change the essential man you are.''

"I know the man I am." He smiled at her, but it was a stubborn smile. "And you don't want a lout like me messing up your life, not even for one night. Don't you see, Anne? It's just the time and the place—Brazil, the jungle, our being here together like this. It's made you vulnerable. But once you're out of this thing, back in New Orleans, you'll wonder how you could have been so crazy to even consider climbing into bed with some river tramp in the Amazon.''

He was infuriating. Couldn't he credit her with enough maturity and common-sense logic to discount the romantic aspects of their situation, to see the reality of their desires? No, obviously he couldn't. It was useless. She couldn't go on sitting here having her pride shredded by his obstinate refusals.

Anne got to her feet, reaching for the tray. "I'll do up the dishes," she said, managing to keep her voice even.

He didn't try to stop her as she headed for the galley.

Anne learned what hell was that night in her cabin.

Hell was lying sleepless in the dark listening to the unnerving beat of rain falling on the deck overhead. Not a brief rain like that afternoon's. This was a steady, prolonged business. She had never heard a lonelier sound.

Hell was wanting the man only a thin wall away from her. Wanting him so desperately that it made her almost sick with longing. And there was nothing she could do about it, even though she could sense his own need on the other side of that wall.

The air was slightly cooler, either because of nightfall or the rain. It made no difference. Anne still felt the heat. Not the heat of the climate but the fever of her own body, a sultry incandescence pulsing demandingly between her thighs. It shocked her, this throbbing desire. She hadn't known she was capable of such forceful passion.

This was what hell was all about, she decided, and it was maddening, senseless. Not one of Ross's arguments mattered. All that counted was what they could give each other, man to woman, woman to man, the very essence of existence. And if this giving and taking had to occur without commitment, she was prepared to settle for that. Why couldn't Ross understand this? Why couldn't he—

And then it struck her. There was something she had neglected to tell him this evening, something so obvious that she couldn't believe she had failed to think of it until now. It made all the difference.

Pride was no longer a consideration as Anne left her tousled bed and headed boldly toward the door. Nor was modesty. She was wearing a light cotton shirt over panties, nothing more. That, too, would have shocked her if she had permitted herself to think about it. She had never played an aggressive role with a man before. But nothing was important except going to Ross, making him understand.

The courage and resolution were there, but she found herself trembling nervously as she approached his cabin door.

Six

There was silence behind Ross's closed door, but Anne was fairly certain that he was awake. Through the wall in her cabin, she had heard him stirring restlessly in his bed, probably as unable to find sleep as she was. And yet she hesitated in the passageway, afraid he would think her a fool or, even worse, a wanton for bursting in on him in the middle of the night.

Then she remembered her resolve, the need to make him understand just how she felt. She lifted her hand and rapped smartly on his door. She didn't wait for his answer. She might have lost her nerve and fled back to her own cabin. Instead, she opened his door and stopped there on the threshold.

His room was in darkness. She couldn't see him, but she heard his sudden movement as he jerked up in bed, surprised by her unexpected appearance.

"Don't turn on the light, Ross," she instructed him, knowing he was groping for the lamp. "And don't talk. Just listen to me, please."

It would be easier saying what she had to say in the anonymous darkness. He was silent and still, complying with her request as he waited for her to go on. She stayed there in the doorway, unable to approach the bed but feeling his awareness of her despite the night's blackness.

Her voice sounded self-consciously throaty as she formed her words. "There's something I need to make clear to you, Ross, something I should have made you understand earlier out on deck. You made a decision for me up there. That's what it amounted to. You made a decision for me, and I sat there and let you do it. Well—" she paused to take a slow, deep breath, and then she struggled on "—that was wrong, all wrong. You have no right to protect me from myself. Only I have that right. I'm not angry about it. It was—was touching of you. But still not right. I'm responsible for me, for risking my own feelings, no one else, and if I choose to be with you . . ."

She paused again, searching for the best way to put it. She could hear his breathing in the thick darkness across the room and knew that he was watching her tensely. But still he said nothing. He wasn't going to make it easy for her. He was going to force her to say it all.

"Ross," she whispered into the blackness, "you don't need to be afraid of the consequences. I won't ask or expect anything but what you're willing to give here and now. That's all I want, just for us to be together."

She stopped. There was no more she could tell him short of begging, and she couldn't bring herself to do that no matter how much she wanted him. The silence was awful. She couldn't stand it.

The response that she waited for so anxiously startled her when it came, not in the form of speech but in action. He turned on the lamp next to his bed. The light dazzled her with its suddenness. Anne gasped softly over the riveting sight it revealed on the bed.

She could tell by the blatant contours of his body that he was naked under the sheet that carelessly covered his lower half. The bared torso above the sheet stunned her with its superb maleness—a bronze physique that was all hard planes and angles, a thicket of matted black hair on his chest that narrowed at the waist and then flared tantalizingly as it met the sheet, a fine sheen of perspiration on his skin that rippled sensuously as he moved, defining his musculature. The perspiration was the result of a body heat that called to her compellingly from across the room.

It was his eyes, though, that Anne finally answered. They were dark and slumberous, and they spoke to her eloquently—the primitive command of a man to a woman. She recognized the forceful summons and obeyed it. She crossed the room slowly and stood by the side of his bed.

The courage and determination that had brought her to his cabin suddenly failed her. She felt dazed, weak in the knees. She realized her need now for a masculine control of the situation. It was his strength that must guide them from this point, his direction.

Still silent, Ross shifted on the bed to make room for her. Anne sank on its edge in gratitude. He leaned toward her, his gaze still locked with hers. There was a film of perspiration on his face that emphasized his pores. It was incredible. Even his pores were sexy to her.

There was no sound but the slow drumming of the rain on the deck overhead, a counterpoint to her rapid heartbeat. The cabin was warm and humid, its sultry air heavy with a suspended urgency. But Ross made no move to touch her. He simply went on looking at her with his hot green eyes, those wonderful eyes that were an inferno consuming her. Why didn't he say something?

He must have read her unspoken plea, and he answered it in a voice deep and rumbling. "It was eating me up lying here wanting you. All I could think about was having you under me, burying myself inside you. And now you're here and I can't stop it. I don't want to stop it. Something tells me I'm going to pay in hell for this, but I just don't care anymore."

"Ross," she whispered, starting to reach for him.

"Slow and easy, sweetheart," he insisted. "Slow and easy. This way..."

Careful not to touch her with his hands or body, nor to permit her to make any similar contact with him, his angled face closed on hers. With the gentlest of pressures, his mouth connected with hers. The tip of his tongue began to lightly caress her lips, tracing their shape from corner to corner. It was the most seductive kiss she had ever experienced. And the most frustrating. She wanted to deepen the kiss, to hold him close. But Ross had already withdrawn his mouth from hers.

"And this..." he said.

His arms still at his sides, he began to plant nipping little kisses on her throat, her cheeks, her forehead. His tongue found the cavity of her ear, teasing it, worrying it. She understood his intention in deliberately holding back. He was creatively, leisurely sensitizing her every nerve ending in order to heighten her passion, to bring her the fullest measure of satisfaction. It was effective since his dewy kisses produced a heavy thickening deep inside her, like warm syrup. But she didn't know how much longer she could endure this massive self-control he was determined to exercise.

The prolonged torment worsened when his hands finally came to life and drifted to the heavy fullness of her breasts, his knuckles barely grazing the undersides through the thin material of her shirt. She shivered as he drew his hands back and forth with feather lightness.

"Ross, please," she pleaded hoarsely.

"Patience, sweetheart. A little patience. We've got the whole night ahead of us."

He demonstrated that one-sided patience by slowly fingering the buttons down the front of her shirt. Anne sat there trembling in sweet torture, yearning for him to simply tear open the shirt. Instead, one by one, he carefully eased the buttons from their holes. When the shirt was finally gaping, he parted the two sides to bring her breasts into full view.

"Look at you," he crooned, his breath quickening with awe at the creamy lushness of her breasts.

Her senses hummed under his drowsy gaze and then went all molten as his head dipped, his face burying into her breasts. His lips closed around a nipple, drawing it deep into his mouth. Anne shut her eyes, arching against him as his sleek tongue moved from peak to peak, spreading liquid fire.

Ross's face was flushed when he finally lifted his head, his breathing harsh. But he refused to abandon his restraint. "We're getting there," he promised. "We're getting there."

And his hand that had been resting at her waist trailed down over the silky tightness of her panties and came to rest against the mound of her womanhood. Gently, slowly, his hand exerted a pressure between her parted thighs as she strained sinuously against the heat and force of his flattened palm.

When Anne could no longer tolerate the roaring in her ears, she collapsed weakly against the solid wall of his chest, moaning softly. He held her without further assault, allowing her a moment of recovery, but the raging inside her would not quit.

The steamy flesh under her cheek gave her no peace, willing her to claim it with her mouth. She turned her head and sought the hollow in his throat, nuzzling it with her nose, bathing it with her tongue. He tasted faintly salty, robustly male, and she couldn't stop until her lips climbed his stubble-roughened jawline and found his mouth, sealing it with hers.

His groan indicated that his self-discipline had been annihilated by her action. His tongue spearing between her lips confirmed it. There was no further attempt to deny, to prolong. The evidence was everywhere—in the raw intensity of his kiss, in his arms dragging her down on the bed beside him, in his blood-heavy manhood pressing its need against her belly.

She had no idea just when and how he rid her of the shirt and panties. Her only awareness was of their sweat-slick bodies in a fantastic embrace, hardness to softness, softness to hardness. Of the rain throbbing on the deck. Of a hunger thick and urgent coiling inside her.

Ross reared over her like a magnificent stallion, then descended slowly, settling between her thighs. His inflamed arousal tenderly, carefully probed the petals of her womanhood.

"Open up for me, sweetheart."

His husky whisper was more of a benediction than a command. It was with that same reverence that the petals unfolded for him, that she drew him deep within the core of her being. She felt a shudder of pleasure course through his long-limbed body as their full unity was achieved.

A mellowness swelled inside her when she heard his guttural, "You feel so good. You're so wet and tight for me."

"Ross," she sighed, stirring under him.

"I know, sweetheart, I know. But let's just feel us for a minute."

She understood. They were motionless, savoring in silence the miracle of their meeting. It was only briefly satisfying. Their bodies demanded the ultimate fulfillment.

Without disturbing their perfect connection, Ross elevated himself above her, supporting his upper weight with arms extended along either side of her, fists planted against the mattress. In this levered position, his hips performed a series of long, slow rotations. The rhythms radiated such waves of heat in Anne that she clutched at his shoulders in desperation, dragging him down against her in the same instant as she thrust up to meet him.

Locked now in a wild tempo, her legs clasping his plunging hips, his deep, blurred voice whispering sweet, earthy endearments, their bodies made a rich passion together. Their souls made a magic.

Passion and magic. They flowed side by side, intermingled, and then were consumed in a frenzied climax. The spasms surged through Anne with such force that she cried out her release in a triumphant joy. Seconds later, Ross's lusty shout expressed his own blinding fulfillment.

Nature rewarded them with a long, lazy euphoria. They lay side by side on the bed, Ross's body cherishing hers with his warm closeness as they listened to the rain that was now as soft and slow as their heartbeats.

It was Ross who interrupted their dreamy intimacy with a low, languid, "Tell me, medicine woman, is there an aphrodisiac that would explain this condition you've reduced me to?"

Anne turned her head, gazing with tenderness at his strong, wonderful face only inches from hers on the pillow they shared. "As far as I know, the industry hasn't developed any reliable aphrodisiac. Why? Are you accusing me of having slipped something into your vegetable soup tonight when you weren't looking?"

With a forefinger, he traced the hairline above her forehead. There was a smile in his eyes and in his voice. "Maybe not. Maybe all it took was the combination of this honey-blond hair and those gray siren's eyes to turn me into helpless mush. You do things to me, lady. You do things to this body of mine that would make a sailor blush just thinking about them."

"You are a sailor," she reminded him with a husky laugh. "And I'm no siren. Medicine woman?"

"Yeah. That's what you do, isn't it? When you're not luring sailors onto sandbars."

"I haven't heard my role in the pharmaceutical world referred to in those terms before, but I guess that is what I do. Only I sell 'em, sailor, I don't mix 'em. Medicines, that is."

"You're proud of that, too, aren't you?"

"Yeah, I am. There's a satisfaction, Ross, in being part of an industry that saves lives and helps people to overcome pain and illness. Like this new drug Richmond has on the market that safely treats certain biochemical depressions. I am proud of that."

"Were you always involved in the family business?"

A serious note had crept into his voice, and she recognized his intent. He wanted to know about her. Lovemaking wasn't just a physical act for him. It involved caring about his partner on a deeper level, and that required understanding her.

Anne was deeply moved by his interest and ready to respond to it. There was only one small problem. He had locked both hands behind his head in an attitude of being prepared to settle back and listen. His casual position with his sleek arm muscles bulging was definitely affecting her libido. Was she unnatural? Could a woman actually be stimulated by the dark, curling hair of a man's underarms?

She couldn't take the chance. Not if they were to talk. She lowered her gaze and managed to calmly answer his ques-

tion. "I wasn't involved at all in the business until well after college. Nor was I interested. I think that was because of
my resentment."

"You resented Richmond Pharmaceuticals?" he asked.

She shook her head. "Not the company itself but my
father's devotion to it. I didn't have a very secure childhood, Ross. Emotionally, that is. I couldn't understand until
I was an adult why my parents didn't have much time for
me. My father was struggling to save a business that, at the
time, wasn't healthy. Neither was his wife. My mother had
a long illness before she died and she didn't deal with it very
well because she'd always been such a strong woman in
every way. Both of them had their hands full, but I couldn't
appreciate that as a child."

"At least you did have a mother."

His words were carelessly spoken, but Anne detected the
bitterness underlying them and felt compassion for him.
"You never knew your mother?"

He shook his head. "She walked out on us when I was too
young to even remember. I heard years later from a cousin
that she'd died. What about your father?"

"He's gone now, too. Sometimes medicines just aren't
enough. But our relationship by that time was a good one.
I'll always be thankful for that."

"No brothers or sisters?"

Anne sighed. "I wish there had been. Maybe I wouldn't
have been so lonely and insecure. My best friend—my only
real friend—was our housekeeper. Carrie is still with me. I
dearly love that lady."

"I can't imagine it. You being lonely and insecure, that
is."

"I was a very different person back then, Ross. I didn't
have any confidence at all. Otherwise, I might not have
minded my situation so much. I was so shy. And painfully
vulnerable."

"Yeah, the vulnerable part I already know."

She gazed at him in wonderment. "Now how could you know that?"

He chuckled. "Because I'm observant."

"Meaning?"

"You have this cute little habit of hugging yourself defensively whenever you're under attack. I know, all right. I've given you cause to hug yourself a lot."

His perceptiveness amazed her. "You're right. I do do that, don't I? I guess I haven't put that old vulnerability behind me after all."

"We're all vulnerable to some degree, Anne. It's just that we have different ways of protecting ourselves. Doesn't mean we lack confidence. So, how did you finally come to find yours?"

Anne hesitated. She wasn't sure that he would appreciate hearing that her ex-husband had to be credited for the first real confidence she ever experienced. "I—I guess it was because of Dane. At least to begin with."

Ross heard the uncertainty in her voice and understood it. "You don't have to worry about telling me, Anne," he assured her gently. "I meant what I said out on deck. I don't see the guy as a threat anymore, but I would like to know why he's still in your life."

"I don't consider that he is."

"You're risking a lot to help him. What do you call that?"

"There's a reason, a good reason."

"Then let me understand it."

Yes, she thought, wanting to confide in him, finding it natural and right to do so. Ross had fascinated her from the start, and he was still fascinating her as she discovered new depths, new strengths in him. This time the insight and sensitivity he was so solicitously offering her not only thrilled her but made it easy to share the emotions of her past.

"Dane and I met in college," she went on to explain. "He was popular, good-looking, and—well, everything I thought I could never be. That's why I was so ecstatic when he cared about me, when he saw qualities in me that I had never seen in myself before."

"Gratitude?"

"Maybe. Except at the time I convinced myself it was love. Who knows? I was so immature back then. Anyway, it felt right at the time. It wasn't until after we were married that I started to see the weaknesses in Dane. He could never seem to settle with anything. He was always into some impractical scheme to make easy money."

"And they failed," Ross guessed.

"Consistently. I did try to believe in him, but it wasn't easy when our finances were forever in a mess. That's why I went to work for Richmond Pharmaceuticals. I wasn't eager to go into the company. I'd started a teaching career for myself, but Dane kept pointing out there was no money in teaching. He was always looking for new investment funds, promising me . . . oh, you get the picture."

"Yeah. The guy was a manipulator."

"So was my father. He'd always wanted me in the business and took advantage of the situation to get me involved with the company. I don't blame them. You can't be manipulated unless you allow it to happen."

"And you did?"

"Yes, to start with."

"What happened then?"

Ross had shifted positions and was turned now on his side facing her. His breath blew softly in her ear. She wished he wouldn't do that. It was decidedly distracting. And arousing.

"Uh, what happened essentially is that I changed and Dane didn't like it."

"How?"

"Well, I surprised myself. I found out that I not only enjoyed my work at Richmond but that I was good at it. Seems that as I came up through the ranks, I proved to have a real executive ability. Suddenly I didn't feel inadequate anymore. The trouble was, the more successful I got as Dad increasingly turned the business over to me because of a heart condition, the more Dane resented it."

"His manipulation backfired on him, huh?"

Ross's warm breath was still disturbing her, this time in the area of her bare shoulder.

"Mmm, you could say that. It put a real strain on the marriage. His ego couldn't take it, I suppose, not when he wasn't succeeding for himself."

"So, the marriage—"

"Broke up in the end, yes."

"Were you hurt?"

"Failure always hurts."

"Does it still hurt, Anne?"

To her relief, Ross's breath was no longer stirring over her sensitized skin. He had drawn back to eye her anxiously because her answer was important to him. She was able to concentrate on her reply.

"You're wondering if I ever really got over him, if that isn't why I'm helping him. Well, I only have one feeling left for Dane—sympathy."

"And maybe a little guilt?" he asked wisely.

"Yes, maybe a little guilt. I can't deny I felt I was failing him somehow when our marriage came apart, that I was at fault, too, even though..." She paused to shake her head unhappily. "Anyway, I guess I do feel responsible for him now out of a sense of guilt. That sounds terrible, doesn't it? Like my only reason for helping him is a selfish one. Something to rid myself of the guilt."

Ross gathered her close, his voice soothing, comforting. "It's a very human and understandable motive, Anne. And don't blame yourself for feeling it when you're making every effort to free him. That's what counts in the end, isn't it?''

"Yes, I suppose so," she agreed, grateful that he had sorted it out for her.

She was also pleased that his breath came again in tingling gusts against her cheek. This time, it wasn't unsettling. Anyway, not until he slid down on the bed and began to sensuously fan her breasts. His warm, moist breath caressed her nipples until they were tight, straining buds. Anne, finding it increasingly difficult to breathe, began to squirm in a sweet delirium.

Ross lifted his head, his expression all innocence. "This bother you?''

"No," she lied. "Why should it? You're not even touching me.''

He grinned at her wickedly. He liked the way she reacted to him, the way her lithe, elegant body went all weak and helpless with desire. "Then maybe,'' he said softly, "it's time I did touch you.''

She didn't object when he captured her lower lip in his mouth, nibbling at its fullness, stroking and tasting it with his tongue. He found the flavor and fragrance of her irresistible. Needing more, he let his tongue slide between her teeth, where he met her tongue, drawing on it, coaxing it.

He stopped kissing her and drew back slightly to look at her. Her face was flushed, her eyes glazed with a mounting passion. It pleased him. But not enough. He wanted to experience her as she had been before, all wild and abandoned and clinging to him.

His hand trailed down over her length, fingers combing through the springy curls above the apex of her thighs. He could feel her stomach clenching with his touch, and when his hand claimed the spot it had been seeking, she began to writhe slowly.

The heat of her directed his fingers in deep, loving motions. She started to moan and buck, and it drove him crazy. He could feel himself swollen and throbbing, the last of his control slipping from him.

"I want you again," he said, hoping his growl sounded sexy to her and not savage. He just couldn't help himself anymore.

She twisted under him, gasping, "The aphrodisiac—"

"Is still working," he promised, sinking against her.

Their joining was as full and satisfying as before, rocking his senses. But his inflamed body permitted no lull this time. Hands supporting the fleshy cheeks of her bottom, he lost himself inside her with long, powerful strokes. He relished the sensation of her nails scoring his back, the feel of her limbs tight around his, her small cries of animal pleasure. They were responses that urged him to a greater effort until he was making love to her with a deep, desperate need that came from the pit of his soul.

Long after Ross had carried them to the pinnacle of fulfillment, he remained inside her, reluctant to disturb their connection even though Anne had drifted off in exhaustion. For the first time in two years, he felt at peace with himself. She had given him something awesome, returned him from a harsh, angry state to a caring, loving one. He would always be grateful for that.

Always. That was the rub. Whatever his serenity of the moment, he doubted that there could be an *always* for them. The demands of their two widely disparate worlds hadn't been resolved by what had happened tonight. Tomorrow, a hard reality would be facing them again. All the conflicts and complications were still waiting for them out there, and maybe they could never be worked out.

He hated this. He didn't know what he was going to do. Whatever her assurance to him about the consequences of tonight, he couldn't simply be a hit-and-run man. It wasn't in his nature. He did feel responsible. He felt responsible not to hurt her, never mind how much he would hurt himself by letting her go. But how was he going to ultimately avoid that when her life waited for her back in New Orleans and his was committed to the jungle and finding Danny?

Ross was afraid for her, and he was afraid for himself.

Seven

She reached out to touch him and he wasn't there.

Feeling a poignant sense of loss, Anne opened her eyes and sat up. Ross was not only gone from the bed but from the cabin. His locker door stood open, indicating he had dressed and taken himself up on deck. The rain had stopped hours ago, and the shimmering light of early morning was invading the cabin with its tropic warmth.

She understood Ross's absence. He would be anxious to check on their situation and to watch for Luiz's return. She wanted to join him, but she was reluctant to leave the bed. The odor of their lovemaking clung to the sheets, kindling sweet memories of last night's potent intimacy.

In the end, realizing she needed to shower and dress before Luiz and his cousins arrived, Anne scooped up her things and returned to her own cabin next door.

She was headed for the shower stall when she caught sight of her face in the mirror above the marble basin. The reflection was revealing and she paused to stare at herself.

Her lips were still red and swollen from Ross's kisses, her cheeks burned from where his beard had rubbed her. A similar evidence of his ardor was on her breasts, which felt ripe and heavy. And there was a soreness between her thighs. A pleasant soreness.

But it was her eyes that held her. Faintly smudged with shadow, they wore the mellow bloom of a woman who, for the first time in her life, had been made to feel complete. Moved, Anne's finger touched the glowing image in the glass. It was then that realization struck her as forcefully as a fist at her windpipe.

She was in love with Ross McIntyre! Hopelessly in love with him! The feeling made her want to laugh and cry at the same time. At some level, she had probably been in love with him almost from the start, though she had never dared to consciously name it. Nor could she properly verbalize it now, not when it deserved the sort of commitment that wasn't yet possible for either of them. Maybe it would never be possible, considering all the difficulties involved, though she dreaded the thought of such an outcome.

And Ross? What was he feeling this morning? She wanted to know and she didn't want to know. Which made her both shy and eager when, showered and dressed, she faced him minutes later in the galley.

He was making breakfast for them. He turned from the stove and smiled at her, his gleaming eyes approving her trim jeans and fresh cotton shirt. "We're having oatmeal. Okay?"

"A heaping bowl for me, please. I'm famished."

"Coming up."

His cheerfulness is encouraging, she thought hopefully as she set the table in the dinette.

"River's up a bit from last night's rain," he reported as he dished up the steaming oatmeal at the table. "Not quite enough to have drifted us off the sandbar, but we might manage a release now with the engine alone."

"That's good," she said.

When they were seated and eating, she waited for him to turn the conversation to a more personal direction. It didn't happen. He went on talking about the boat, teasingly complimenting her for grounding them without any noticeable tilt to the vessel.

The brightness was still in his eyes and in his smile, but she began to sense that there was a melancholy behind it. Anne realized he had no intention of discussing their situation, of even referring to last night, no matter how desperately she wanted it. Ross was not going to convey his feelings for her. He was not going to tell her he loved her.

She could do nothing but accept his decision. She had given herself no other choice when she had promised him that there would be no consequences, no demand on his emotions. She understood his inner melancholy. Ross was the kind of man who would think that he was failing her with his silence, yet he wasn't able to deal with the subject of commitment.

Maybe he's right, she decided. Maybe it didn't make sense trying to untangle their relationship until the risks and frustrations of this voyage were behind them. And what then? What if Ross was never able to give her anything more than last night?

The possibility was unbearable, but she couldn't blame him. He had warned her against any involvement with him. So, where did that leave her? No place, she realized unhappily.

But he didn't deserve her despondency. She owed him the same safe morning-after amiability he was offering her.

"No sign of Luiz yet, huh?" she asked him pleasantly.

She saw relief in Ross's eyes. He was grateful that she didn't intend to press him. There was admiration and respect there, too, and for now, that would have to be enough.

"It's early," he assured her. "He'll get here."

"Ross, what if Luiz and the men aren't able—"

"Listen," he interrupted her, holding up his hand for silence.

Anne sat motionless, and then after a few seconds, she heard it, too. The sound of an engine. "There he is now."

Ross said nothing. He was suddenly grim-faced.

"Ross, what is it?"

He got up from the table, reaching for his cap. "Come on."

Mystified, she followed him out on deck. They went to the stern and hung over the rail, scanning the river upstream. There was no sign yet of any craft, but the sound of the engine was louder. It must be close, she thought. Probably just around the next bend.

Anne glanced at Ross. His face was still tight with concern. And then, listening more closely to the throb of the approaching engine, she understood. This wasn't the putt-putt of an outboard leading a flotilla of dugouts. This was the powerful engine of a larger craft.

Ross turned to her with a decisive, "Whatever happens, let me handle it. Just don't question anything. Will you promise me that?"

"Not until you tell me what's wrong."

"Anne, we have gold on board and we're caught here. Remember?" She doesn't need to know any more than that, he thought. He wasn't going to tell her that from the moment they had left Manaus, he had been worried about what they were carrying in her cabin, of knowledge of the safe's contents somehow reaching the wrong people. This was the Amazon, and river piracy and its ugly consequences weren't unknown.

Anne, understanding, gulped fearfully and nodded. "All right, but couldn't it be just another ordinary boat like ours?"

"Maybe." But his instinct was telling him otherwise.

They waited tensely at the rail and minutes later, the prow of what was unmistakably a gunboat nosed around the bend in the river and headed straight toward them.

Anne's hands gripped the rail. "Is it—"

Ross shook his head. "It's a military patrol."

She wilted in relief, expecting Ross to do the same. But when she looked at him he was far from relaxed. "Isn't it all right?" she asked.

"The same instructions apply. Let me handle it."

She didn't argue. He must have his reason and she trusted his judgment and experience. They watched in silence as the gunboat cut its engine, anchoring well away from the sandbar. There was a small flurry of activity on its deck.

"That's Luiz with them," she murmured in surprise.

"Yes, and they're lowering our outboard over the side."

The small outboard began to slice through the water toward the *Lady Odyssey*. Luiz was operating it. He was accompanied by an older man in a crisp khaki uniform.

When the outboard reached the stern of the yacht, the uniformed officer came to his feet and hailed Ross in polite, flawless English. "May I come on board?"

"You know you're always welcome, Colonel Pereira."

Ross knew the man, Anne realized. And their exchange had been a friendly one. Then what was bothering him? Deciding to follow his example of caution, she watched the action carefully and was rewarded for her observation.

As the agile officer clambered to the deck, Luiz, from behind him, met Ross's inquiring gaze and answered it with an expressive shake of his head. His silent message was clear. He was saying he had been questioned but had revealed nothing.

Colonel Pereira, reaching the deck, shook hands with Ross. "As luck would have it, *Capitão*," he explained, "we met your man in the village. When he informed us of your trouble, I insisted we come to your rescue ourselves. The dugouts of his friends would have been useless, I'm afraid."

"That was good of you, Colonel. But last night's rain might let us ease off this thing under our own power."

"In any case, we will stand by until you're free." He turned his head, eyeing Anne with interest.

"My passenger, Anne Richmond," Ross introduced her.

Anne found herself confronting a stocky man with shrewd black eyes, strong features and a graying moustache. "My pleasure, Senhora Richmond." He didn't seem surprised to find her on board.

Anne acknowledged the introduction with a smile while noticing Luiz hovering nervously in the background behind the colonel. He was plainly anxious about something. Ross noticed it, too, and started to edge toward his deck hand.

She made it her business to distract the officer while Ross spoke privately to Luiz. "Colonel, we have fresh coffee. Can I offer you a cup? Or maybe something cool?"

"Thank you, no, but I will sit."

As she led him toward the deck chairs, she could hear Luiz's quick, excited mutter to Ross. Something was definitely up. Pereira had to be just as aware of their whispered exchange, but he didn't react to it as they settled in the chairs.

Anne found herself liking the colonel. There was a straightforward, cordial manner about him. But she didn't relish the idea of making small talk while Ross conferred with Luiz. It turned out to be unnecessary. The deck hand went off to the galley, and Ross joined them almost immediately. He stood with casual ease against the rail, though there was an alertness in his eyes. She sensed trouble.

"So, Colonel," Ross asked, "what's a high-ranking officer doing way up here along the Jara? Inspecting the patrol boats maybe?"

"Not this time, my friend. I am after big game."

"Thought that was illegal, except for the Indians."

"Ah, but I do have Indian blood in me. Enough of it to give me the instincts of a jungle tracker."

"Any luck?"

The officer spread his hands in a gesture indicating failure. "Not as yet, but I have hopes. I don't give up, because this game I am hunting needs to be found and captured."

"A real nuisance, huh?"

"When it raids the government shipping and makes the rivers and forest unsafe, I would say yes." He turned his shrewd eyes on Anne. "I am sure you have heard of the People's Liberation Army, *senhora*."

Anne tensed. This was why Ross had warned her to say nothing. "Guerrilla rebels, aren't they?"

"This is what the band calls itself," the colonel said in contempt. "Their activities are more criminal, however, than political."

"Well, I wouldn't know anything about that."

The officer's eyes hardened. "I find that rather curious, *senhora*, considering your ex-husband is a guest of the People's Liberation Army."

It was Ross who answered the colonel, his voice totally bland. "Now where did you hear a wild rumor like that?"

"A reliable source, *Capitão*."

Ross shook his head. "Afraid you've been misinformed, Colonel."

Pereira arched one eyebrow and smiled. "Then I wonder why Senhora Richmond is aboard the *Lady Odyssey* if not to carry a ransom to free the man the revolutionaries are holding hostage."

Ross smiled back at him in confidence. "Ms. Richmond is here to study jungle medicines for her company. There's no ransom."

"My contact at the bank in Manaus where the ransom was obtained tells me otherwise. A quantity of gold, I believe, in the form of Krugerrands."

Anne felt her insides tighten. Did he have the authority to search the yacht, find the gold in her cabin? Just what did he want from them?

She looked to Ross for the answer and was surprised and confused by what she saw. The skipper's cap, his own badge of authority aboard the *Lady Odyssey*, was back on his head as he slowly straightened at the rail. She had learned to determine his moods by the way he wore that cap, just as she had learned to read the body language of the people she worked with in the pharmaceutical industry. When he angled the cap to the back of his head, it meant he was relaxed, amused. When he tilted it to one side, you could expect him to be reflective or inquisitive. When he tugged it forward, shading his narrowed eyes, it indicated his displeasure. But this time he was wearing it perfectly level on his head. She didn't know what that signified, though she soon found out.

"Afraid you're on the wrong track this time, Colonel. There's no gold on board." He was still smiling.

Pereira sighed, his gaze trained appealingly on Anne. "I'm sorry to hear that. I was hoping, *senhora*, that you would help us to catch the rebels. I was hoping that, when you delivered the ransom, you would be willing to lead us to the camp we have been unable to locate. I was hoping that you would want these outlaws captured as they have captured and held your ex-husband."

It was then she realized what the cap's position on Ross's head expressed—a canny innocence. He was prepared to outmaneuver Colonel Pereira. "Now that's interesting, Colonel, what you want Ms. Richmond to do for you. Because if she were on such a rescue mission as you describe—which, as I've told you, she is definitely not—but *if* she were on such a mission, then the kind of operation you propose to involve her in would be awfully risky. Downright dangerous for her, in fact. You consider that?"

"Precautions would be exercised."

"Uh-huh. Well, that would be tricky to manage in a situation like this, wouldn't it? Not at all reliable. Then there's the threat to this—who did you say?—ex-husband they're supposed to be holding. Seems to me if they've got a hostage and they figure they're being betrayed, they would end up executing the guy before you could rescue him. I mean, it's a strong possibility."

Colonel Pereira nodded with a slow, reluctant smile. "You make your point, *Capitão*."

"Yeah, I thought you'd appreciate it. But look, Colonel, if we should somehow happen to stumble on this rebel camp of yours—you know, while Ms. Richmond is researching jungle medicines—you've got my promise, we'll tell you all about it just as soon as we're safely out of there."

"That's very generous of you, my friend." The colonel was thoughtful for a few seconds and then he got to his feet. "Now I must return to the gunboat. I have other business downriver. We will wait, of course, until you are free of the sandbar." He turned to Anne. "I trust, Senhora Richmond, that you will be very careful when you are studying jungle medicines."

"I intend to be, Colonel," she assured him.

Minutes later, Anne and Ross stood at the rail watching Luiz ferry the officer back to the gunboat.

"You know," she told him softly, "I haven't seen a piece of guileless strategy work that effectively in an executive boardroom. McIntyre, you're wasting your talents out here in the bush."

"You were impressed, huh?"

"I was, but I don't think Colonel Pereira was happy about your sneaky performance."

"No, but if I'd refused outright to be cooperative, he might have left us hung up on this sandbar. This way, without real proof, he has no choice but to play it our way."

"He might have searched the boat and found the gold."

"We could still have refused him and he knew that." Ross pushed away from the rail. "Well, time to fire up the engine. Let's hope we get off this thing without needing their help. I want that gunboat on its way and out of sight."

"Why?"

"Because of what Luiz told me while you were entertaining Pereira."

She noticed that his jaw had tightened grimly. "Ross—"

"Later," he insisted, heading for the wheelhouse.

To Anne's relief, what the *Lady Odyssey*'s engine had been unable to accomplish yesterday afternoon was now achieved with little effort. The sandbar released them.

As the yacht swung around to pick up Luiz and the outboard, the watching gunboat signaled its approval and sped on its way, disappearing around a bend downriver.

"Now tell me," Anne pleaded.

Ross turned from the davits where he had been raising and securing the outboard. His expression was still tense. "This is it. The rebel contact."

"How? When?"

"Luiz was approached in the village this morning just before the gunboat arrived. They sent an Indian guide out to meet us. He's waiting now."

"In the village?"

"No, at an isolated inlet a few miles upriver from the village. Luiz knows the spot. Anne, they're not going to settle for an exchange on the river. They'll accept nothing but an on-the-spot trade at the camp itself. It means going into the jungle. A long way."

"And?"

"I'll do it. I'll take the ransom and go with their man."

"Ross, no. Listen to me, please. This isn't your—"

"No arguments. You'll wait at the boat with Luiz."

The *Lady Odyssey* plowed upriver, passing the village where Luiz had spent the night. Anne stood at the bow rail, frustration simmering inside her. Ross McIntyre, she decided, was an exasperatingly stubborn male, his attitude in this situation as archaically macho as that of the native men along the river. He was also slightly wonderful. He was determined to protect her, of course, and for that she was touched and grateful, though still resenting his abrupt orders. She hadn't stopped to argue with him, however. Not when it was so important to reach this guide. But in her mind, the question of just who was to accompany the guide had yet to be settled.

The meeting place had been well chosen by the rebels. The opening for the inlet to which Luiz directed them was so screened by vegetation that it was known only by a few locals. The yacht had to butt its way through a curtain of overhanging fronds to gain access to the long channel beyond.

The waterway wound into the jungle itself, a green corridor of arching palms, matted vines and a profusion of sweet blossoms like small white moons. The packed growth closed behind them as they crawled along the twisting inlet, and Anne found herself holding her breath. There was an otherworld stillness about the hushed tunnel that, for all its primitive beauty, made her uneasy. Even the yacht's engine seemed to throb more softly. The heat, away from the open river, was intense.

Anne was alone on the deck. Luiz was in the wheelhouse with Ross, who was negotiating the narrow passage with every care. She could see the deckhand assuring him that the channel was deep and safe all the way. Luiz had fished here as a boy.

The Jara was only a memory by the time the tight inlet widened into a basin whose curious green depths were shot with rippling sunlight. Ross, avoiding a choking tangle of purple water hyacinths, cut the engine and coasted the vessel to a steeply sloping bank.

The anchor went down and, in the silence that followed, Anne could hear the drone of insects and the call of a bird. The men joined her on deck, and from out of nowhere appeared their Indian guide.

He was a startling sight standing there on the shore, watching them impassively. A fringe of glossy black hair came down over the brown forehead of his round face. Red feathers were in his pierced ears and nose. And along with the feathers and the fruit dye painted on his cheeks, he was wearing a Walt Disney World T-shirt.

"Where do you suppose he ever came by that shirt?" Anne asked.

Ross shrugged. "Who knows? They'll trade for all kinds of strange stuff. His name is Kona. Luiz thinks he's a Yanomamo, though this isn't their territory. Not the most pleasant people, but apparently the rebels trust this one. Come on, time to communicate."

This proved to be a complicated task, as Ross quickly discovered when they joined the Indian on the bank. Kona's version of Portuguese didn't seem to match his. Luiz had better luck interpreting the guide's dialect and ended up translating the long exchange.

Anne understood none of the discussion as she waited impatiently, but one thing was very clear. Neither side was agreeing with the other. The Indian grunted what could only be negative responses while Ross, looking unhappier by the moment, kept Luiz busy with fresh appeals.

In the end, Ross turned to her with a sigh of defeat. "It's no good. His orders are to bring you personally to the camp, along with the gold, and he won't have it any other way. Not only will he not accept me as a substitute, but we had a devil of a time convincing him that I'm coming along. I made it clear you weren't going anywhere without me. He's not too thrilled about that, but I gave him no choice."

Anne was not surprised by the outcome of the argument. She hadn't forgotten that the ransom letter had specified that she bring the gold herself.

"I don't understand it," Ross said, shaking his head. "As long as they get the Krugerrands, what difference does it make who brings them?"

"Maybe they're afraid anyone else but me might be the authorities moving in on them. Anyway, it doesn't matter. I'm prepared to go."

"Yeah, but I'm not prepared to have you go. The jungle isn't a friendly place, Anne."

"It's all right," she assured him, trying to tease him out of his grimness. "I had all my shots against tropical diseases before I left the States."

"There's no inoculation, Anne, for the bite of a fer-de-lance or a mauling by a wild boar. But since there's no helping it, we'd better collect our stuff and move out. Kona says the camp is several hours' walk from here."

While the Indian squatted on the bank and patiently waited, they returned to the yacht to gather the essentials. The gold coins were removed from the safe and placed in a backpack that Ross strapped to his shoulders. Luiz filled a pair of canteens with fresh water while Anne fastened a small first-aid kit to her belt.

Minutes later, Ross and Anne were back on shore and following the silent Kona along a narrow trail. The jungle swallowed them almost immediately, and Luiz and the *Lady Odyssey* were lost to sight.

Anne found that actually being inside the rain forest was a far different experience than observing it from the river. It was awesome—and sinister—in its primordial splendor. Except for the thread of the trail, the growth was impenetrable on all sides—a sprawling wilderness of rough-barked palm, towering boles of balsa and clinging webs of garlic vine. With monkeys chittering overhead and the brilliant flash of parakeets, it was hard to remember that somewhere on this same planet were such things as electronics-age cities and crowded freeways.

In the beginning, she was grateful for the solid canopy of foliage high overhead. It blocked out the fierce equatorial sun, creating a perpetual twilight on the forest floor where the sweet-sour odor of rotting vegetation overwhelmed the senses. But after a while, she began to long for the honest swelter of the sun. The jungle was like an airless hothouse, making every breath an effort.

"I didn't realize it would be so oppressive in here," she said.

"It's all the growth," Ross explained. "It sweats into the air."

It's not just the plants that are sweating, she thought. She was uncomfortably aware of the perspiration that trickled between her breasts and pasted damp tendrils of her blond hair to her ears and neck.

The sticky wetness attracted mosquitoes, which swarmed around them ferociously. She and Ross had liberally doused themselves with insect repellant, but it did little to discourage them. Anne was kept busy swatting and slapping.

She could see Ross was miserable, too. His shirt was stained with sweat and he softly cursed the clouds of insects. The straps of the backpack seemed to be cutting into his shoulders. The gold was heavy.

"I could take a turn with the backpack," she offered.

"Forget it. I like to suffer."

"*He* isn't minding anything, though, is he?" Anne indicated their guide marching on the path ahead of them. Kona seemed impervious to both the bugs and the heat. He also ignored his two charges, never pausing to check on their welfare or their progress.

"It's his world. He's used to it. Look at him. He never looks back. He just goes on and assumes we're right here behind him. Which we'd damn well better be. If we ever lost him in here..."

Anne shuddered at the prospect. "We'd never get out, would we?"

"Not when you consider all those other trails we've been crossing. There's a regular maze of them. Pereira can forget our ever trying to describe the route to him once we get back. The rebels are no fools."

Anne knew what he meant. For all its savage, unique beauty, there was a bewildering sameness about the jungle, unrelieved as it was by a single clearing. In time, the unchanging monotony began to nag at her. She felt limp and tired.

"Ross, do you think we could get him to stop for a few minutes? I don't know about you, but I'm ready for a break."

"Good idea, but we can't just drop to the ground. The ants would eat us alive."

As they moved on, he searched for a safe place to rest. He found it a few minutes later in the form of a tree whose enormous girth was thick with buttressed roots that were as good as stools.

Ross signaled to Kona, making him understand with gestures that they needed to rest. Then, before he would allow Anne to sit, Ross checked carefully between the roots, making certain there were no lurking reptiles. Satisfied, he handed her one of the canteens. Anne sank with relief onto one of the roots.

Kona didn't join them and refused the offer of water for himself. He hunkered down on the path several paces away and proceeded to doze.

"How far do you think we've come?" she asked.

Ross checked his watch. "I wouldn't begin to guess it in miles, but it looks like we have about an hour or so ahead of us yet."

She nodded and uncapped her canteen, sipping gratefully. The water was tepid, but it did refresh her. She glanced at Ross seated on the root next to hers. He wasn't bothering with his own canteen. He was gazing off into the forest, a hypnotic, faraway expression in his eyes. Anne knew immediately what was on his mind.

He's thinking about his son, she told herself. He's remembering Danny, lost out there somewhere in all this wildness. And it's killing him wondering about the boy.

She had promised herself this morning that she was not going to examine her relationship with Ross until the treacherous expedition was behind them. But how could she not consider the future when their arrival at the camp was imminent, when there was the fear of how they would be treated by the rebels? If the worst should happen, if everything ended for them there, she wanted the assurance that it had all been worthwhile, that what she had shared with Ross was more than just a night of intimacy.

But she couldn't offer herself that assurance. She couldn't count on any potential "forevers" for them because Ross was a man who was possessed. Whether it made sense or not, he would never abandon his search for the boy. He would stay down here forever, seeking his son. And even if, somehow, she contrived to remain with him in Brazil, how could they ever achieve happiness when a part of him would always be yearning for his missing son, his despair and guilt eating at his soul?

She understood. If the situation were reversed, if it were her child who was missing, she would react in exactly the same way. Ross had no choice about his determination. And she wouldn't love him if he did.

And she had to face that Ross had never said he loved her, had never indicated that last night was anything more than a matter of plain lust for him.

"Ready to move on?" he asked, interrupting her thoughts.

"Yes, I feel better."

His hand came to her elbow, guiding her to her feet.

No, she decided with a quick smile of satisfaction, it had been much more than just lust for him. No man could be as quietly, tenderly protective of a woman as he had been of her all day, unless his feelings for her ran deep. His hand unnecessarily at her elbow was evidence of that. All through the long trek, he had been watching over her like this, his fingers steadying her when she stumbled over roots, his hand on her arm or back gently steering her away from anything he regarded as suspicious on the path. Anne didn't need his assistance, but she welcomed his touches as though they were caresses.

It's his way of cherishing me, she realized. And if that wasn't love, it was some form of special caring and for now, it would have to be enough.

It was Ross's sharp-eyed concern for her safety that prevented Anne from hiding the pain in her right leg minutes later along the trail.

"You're limping," he accused her. The narrowness of the path at this point had forced him to drop behind her. He had immediately noticed her uneven gait.

She tried to move on without answering him, but his hand caught her and swung her around to face him. "What's wrong?" he demanded.

"I—I don't know. My leg hurts a little, that's all."

"Since when?"

"Not long. Maybe since we left the tree."

"Why didn't you say something?"

"I—well, I didn't think it was anything important. I just wanted us to get on to the camp and then—"

"So, you not only didn't mention it, you didn't even pause to look at it." He was angry with her. He admired her spirit, all she was enduring without a whimper, but this was carrying courage too far. "Damn it, Anne, you don't have to be so brave. You're entitled to an honest complaint."

"I'm not being brave. It's just that I'm not used to walking so far and my legs are sore."

"Bull! It's more than that. Look at you. You're white and wilting. What happened? Did you twist your ankle maybe?"

"No, nothing like that. Nothing happened."

"Well, something is wrong and we're not waiting for the camp to check it." He crouched down on the path in front of her. "Roll up your pant leg," he ordered.

Anne obeyed him. He leaned toward the leg, inspecting it. The flesh was tender along the side of her calf and when he touched her there, she sucked in her breath in sharp pain. She tried to see the area for herself, but his head was in the way.

"It's red and swollen there," he reported. She didn't care for the grimness in his voice.

"It does feel a bit raw," she admitted.

"I think you've been bitten. My guess would be a spider. Can't you remember it happening?"

How could she remember any particular insect sting when, from the moment they had entered the jungle, she had been suffering from every flying, crawling, slithering torment imaginable? "Ross, look at me. I'm covered with welts that I've been scratching ever since we started walking. I don't remember any special bite. I remember *all* of them."

He nodded. "It must have been back at the tree, something there in the roots we didn't notice."

"Do—do you think it was a poisonous spider?" she asked fearfully.

"Anne, I don't know." She could see he was worried by the wound, and suddenly she was worried, as well. They were virtually helpless out here in the jungle, far away from any medical aid.

Ross looked up. Kona had stopped on the trail ahead and was watching them with indifference. Ross motioned the guide to join them, pointing to the swelling on Anne's leg and trying in Portuguese to ask the Indian's opinion. Kona merely shrugged after glancing at the leg.

Ross cursed under his breath. "Let's have the first-aid kit." Anne unfastened the kit from her belt and handed it to him. He examined the contents and then shook his head. "There's nothing in here to treat a spider bite. Nothing I'd want to risk, anyway."

"I'm a fine advertisement for a pharmaceutical company, aren't I?" she said, trying to make light of a situation that scared her.

Ross glared at her, in no mood for her teasing.

"Look, I'll be okay," she assured him. "The camp can't be that far and once we get there, someone is bound to help. Way off in the jungle like this, they may even have their own doctor. I can make it, Ross."

He got to his feet, his face determined. "You're not walking on that leg. If there is poison in there, further movement would only spread it. I'm carrying you."

"Ross, no. You can't possibly carry me when you're already carrying the gold, and the distance—"

"Quiet," he insisted.

Before she could stop him, he had swung her into his arms and was striding up the path behind Kona. Anne offered no further objections. The leg was throbbing now and she feared it wouldn't support her for any length of time.

Besides, she couldn't deny the wonderful sense of security she felt cradled in his strong arms. His chest was hard and warm under her cheek, and even the sweaty male aroma of him was reassuring. After a time, however, listening to his labored breathing, she feared her weight was exhausting him.

"If we could find a strong branch," she suggested, "I could use it as a crutch. I'm sure I could manage that way without putting any strain on the leg. Ross—"

His only reply was to tighten his arms around her more firmly. It was pointless to argue. He wasn't going to listen.

They pushed on, and Anne began to long for the end of the trail. But the lush vegetation gave no sign of thinning. There was never a glimpse of sunlight promising a clearing. The leg went on aching.

She must have drowsed against his chest. The next thing she knew, they were stopped on the trail and she could feel Ross's body suddenly turn rigid and alert.

She opened her eyes. The path had widened, and in front of them was an almost blinding glare. But that wasn't what startled her. It was the alarming sight of being silently surrounded by a half dozen men with the dispassionate, hardened faces of guerrilla fighters. They wore tattered jungle fatigues, and the weapons they pointed at Anne and Ross were lethal assault rifles.

Eight

Guarded by the rebels who had intercepted them on the path, Anne and Ross were led into the source of the glare. They had arrived at the camp clearing.

"I suppose we had no right to expect our reception would be a friendly one, even if we were expected," Ross muttered.

One of the men barked an order and Ross came to a halt.

"What is he saying?" Anne whispered anxiously. "Could you understand him?"

"Yeah, his Portuguese I can follow. He's telling us to wait right here. They're going for their leader."

Two of the men went off toward a hut at the other end of the clearing, leaving the other four to watch Anne and Ross. The rifles were no longer aimed at them, but the guards continued to look at them suspiciously, even though they had checked them for weapons. Kona, his duty performed, had slipped away.

The sun beating down on them was merciless, and Ross was still bearing Anne's weight. "Ross, put me down. I can stand."

When he offered no objection, Anne realized how exhausted he was. He lowered her carefully to the ground, but he kept an arm around her waist, supporting her.

"They might have let us wait out of the sun," Anne grumbled.

Ross nodded in agreement. "There's no shortage of shade. You notice how they left plenty of trees standing? Camouflage so they can't be spotted easily from the air."

"You think they built this camp as their headquarters, then?"

He shook his head. "They must keep on the move to avoid capture. My guess is they've temporarily taken over an abandoned Indian village. It's a primitive setup, all these grass huts."

Anne wondered where they were holding Dane. There was no sign of him among the men in the clearing, most of whom were stretched out in hammocks and paying no attention to the new arrivals as they rested in the midday heat.

There was a long silence except for the lazy drone of insects. Anne tired to ignore the burning in her leg.

The two men finally reappeared at the entrance to the hut. They were followed by a third man hastily buttoning a ragged tunic. He strutted toward them like a bantam rooster. When he reached them, he grinned cheerfully, displaying a mouth full of gold crowns.

He addressed them in Portuguese, and Anne waited impatiently through the long exchange he had with Ross.

"What's he saying?" she finally demanded.

"His name is Emmanuel Vargas. He's the headman here, and he welcomes us to his camp."

"He seems friendly enough, an improvement over the others."

"So far. I said we needed help for your leg. He's sending for someone. Come on." Ross scooped her up into his arms again.

"Where are we going?"

"Out of the sun."

Vargas led the way toward a large, open-sided shelter in the center of the clearing. Anne thought the sagging, palm-thatched structure might have been a kind of common meetinghouse for the Indians who must have built it. It was a relief to have Ross gently place her on a rough cot that was waiting there.

"Did you ask him about Dane?"

Ross nodded. "Also being sent for. But Vargas made it clear none of us is leaving here until he's counted the Kruger-rands. I made it just as clear that I don't hand over the gold until we're sure the man we've come for is in one piece. He assures me Dane is whole and healthy. He's off with his guard at some nearby stream where they allow him to take a daily bath."

They went on waiting in the shelter. Ross, perched on the edge of the cot where Anne was stretched out resting her leg, fanned away the flies that tried to settle on both of them. There was only one guard with them now, so young he was hardly more than a boy. He leaned against a nearby post, rifle slung over his shoulder as he proceeded to look bored.

Vargas had also disappeared, but within minutes he was crossing the clearing toward them. He was accompanied by another young soldier in worn fatigues. This one turned out to be a woman, slim and doe-eyed.

When they arrived at the shelter, she crouched at the side of Anne's cot. "I speak English," she informed them kindly. "My name is Elena. Vargas has asked that I look at your leg."

"Are you a doctor?" Ross asked hopefully, moving off the cot to give her room.

Elena shook her head. "We have no doctor here and almost nothing in the way of medical supplies. But I have some skill in treating wounds and illnesses. If you will raise your pant leg, I will see what can be done."

Anne nodded and rolled the jeans above her knee, exposing the injured leg.

Elena leaned forward, inspecting the inflammation that had now swollen and reddened the entire calf of the leg. "*Santo Madre,*" she breathed at the sight of the infection. "What happened here?"

"We think a spider bite," Anne said, "but we don't know what kind."

"Can you help her?" Ross asked, the worry evident in his voice.

Elena got to her feet, nodding slowly. "I can try. There is an Indian remedy I know of to heal such infections. I must go into the jungle to collect what I need. It will not take long."

She left the shelter. Vargas, sober-faced now, went with her.

When they were alone again, Ross held up one of the canteens. "Are you thirsty?"

"Yes, please." Anne reached for the canteen he offered.

"It's going to be okay, Anne," he assured her solemnly.

Touched by his gentle promise, she accepted the canteen with a soft smile. "I know."

He watched her uncap the canteen and start to drink. The water never touched her lips. She had suddenly forgotten the canteen in her hand and was staring off across the clearing. Ross turned around to see what captured her attention.

A tall, athletic figure with an armed rebel trailing after him was striding toward the shelter. Ross didn't have to be told that this was Dane Matthews.

Yes, he could see why Anne had once fallen for the guy. Even in slacks and a polo shirt that were grubby and torn from his ordeal and with his dark blond hair needing a barber's attention, he projected the smooth good looks of the hotshot photojournalist he was trying to be.

Ross told himself not to resent the man. After all, he must have suffered something waiting for them to reach him. He was certainly overjoyed at the sight of them. Or at the sight of Anne, anyway.

Reaching the shelter, Dane dropped at the side of the cot. "Anne! I knew you'd come! I knew you wouldn't let me down!"

Anne searched his face. "Are you all right, Dane? They didn't hurt you?"

"I'm okay. They were decent enough to me, even let me keep my camera and film as long as I didn't record anything here. When it suits them, they're anxious to look like the good guys. It's you I'm worried about." He reached for her hand, squeezing her fingers. "What's wrong? They said something happened to you in the jungle."

Ross answered with a quiet, "Probably a spider bite. The girl, Elena, thinks she can help her."

Dane looked up at Ross, then down at Anne again. Ross could see he was wondering about him. Anne introduced the two men. "This is Ross McIntyre, Dane. He brought me up from Manaus on his boat. He—he helped me to reach you."

Dane stood and the two men shook hands. Ross noticed that the photojournalist hadn't missed Anne's hesitation in explaining him. "Then I'm grateful to you, McIntyre."

Ross nodded. "Exactly how did you get yourself in this fix, anyway?"

Dane shrugged. "A lot of bad judgment. The first was in hiring an Indian guide who had us all over the map before running out on me just as we landed in the rebel camp."

"Didn't you anticipate these people might grab you?"

"Hell, I thought they'd be pleased that I wanted to do a sympathetic coverage on them, let the world know who they are and what they're fighting for. Okay, so I was naive, but I needed the break." He crouched beside the cot again, appealing to Anne. "You understand that, don't you, Annie? You know I wouldn't have gotten you involved in this mess if I could have avoided it. But when they searched me and found the snapshot of us in my wallet— You remember that picture, don't you?" He flashed a persuasive smile, reaching for her hand again. "The one with the two of us standing in front of my college dorm. I still carry it."

"I remember."

"Well, they asked me questions. A lot of questions. They asked me about you. I was scared and not thinking straight. I thought it would help my case if I told them about the good work your company is doing through its branch in Manaus. I figured they'd be impressed you're trying to help the people they claim they're fighting for. Turns out that what impressed them was your money. Can you forgive me, Annie?"

He wants her, Ross suddenly realized, watching Dane's eagerness. He wants her back again and he thinks he stands the chance of getting her. He's convinced himself that her being here for him is evidence that she still cares.

Ross had another unpleasant thought then. Maybe it hadn't been important to the rebels that Anne come in person to buy the release of their captive. Why should it matter to them who brought the gold as long as they got it? But to Dane, it could have been an excuse to bring Anne back into his life and he might have influenced their ransom instructions. If so, then he was a bastard for endangering her like this.

"It's okay, Dane," Anne assured him. "I have what they asked for and with any luck, we'll soon be out of here."

But Emmanuel Vargas, returning just then with Elena, refused to discuss their release until the gold was in his possession. He had been eyeing the backpack ever since their arrival, deciding that's where the coins had to be, and he was obviously impatient to claim them. Only after Ross had secured the rebel leader's promise that he would provide them with a stretcher for Anne, along with Kona to guide them back to the river, did he remove the backpack and pass it to Vargas.

With the gold finally in his hands, the pompous little man nodded at Elena, granting his permission to treat the leg.

Elena knelt at the side of the cot, a basket in her hands. ''This will do you no harm,'' she explained, ''but I cannot guarantee it will cure you, either. Are you willing?''

Anne nodded. ''Go ahead.''

Dane hovered over the cot as Elena proceeded with the treatment. But Ross, understanding the tension Anne was experiencing, didn't want to add to her discomfort by remaining close to the cot where she could sense his concern and uncertainty. Lounging against a nearby upright, hands thrust into his pockets, he tried to look as casual as possible. But all the while he prayed that Elena knew what she was doing and that this wasn't some worthless witch doctor's remedy.

''These are merely cobwebs I am placing over the swelling,'' Elena instructed her patient as she worked. ''And this I am sprinkling on the cobwebs are spores gathered from toadstools in the forest.''

''Jungle medicine,'' Anne said, unable to help her fascination. ''I'll have to remember to tell Richmond's research lab about this.''

She looked up, automatically seeking Ross's gaze, wanting to share the moment with him. She found him standing against the post. Ross knew his casual pose was no good. She was instantly able to read the tightness in his jaw, the solicitude for her in his eyes. She flashed him a brief, reassuring smile and then became absorbed again in Elena's treatment.

Ross felt another gaze on him then. Dane was watching him. He hadn't missed the meaningful exchange with Anne. Ross knew the photojournalist had been puzzled by his relationship with Anne from the moment he had found them together in the shelter. He could see that Dane understood it now. He realized they were lovers and what's more, he didn't like it one bit.

Ross's eyes met the other man's. He longed to send a silent message to Matthews, a possessive and challenging, *Keep off. You lost her, and she's mine now.* But he didn't have that right. Anne didn't belong to him, and maybe she never could.

Hating the situation almost as much as he hated himself for failing to be what he believed Anne needed, he allowed his gaze to shift away from Dane's. Whatever had to be sorted out and settled, this wasn't the moment for it.

Elena was just finishing the application on the leg when there was a sudden uproar off the far edge of the clearing. Startled, they heard the angry shouts of sentries and the crashing of bodies through the thick vegetation. A shot rang out, followed by a hoarse cry. Vargas, who had been checking the gold at the other end of the shelter, sprang to his feet, reaching for the handgun in his belt. The other rebels tumbled out of their hammocks, clutching rifles as they joined their leader, who was now charging toward the commotion.

Ross had moved toward Anne at the first sign of trouble. If this was some form of surprise attack, he meant to shield her. He never reached her side. The young guard who had remained with them in the shelter leveled his rifle at him, warning him to stay where he was. Ross had no choice but to back off and wait with the others through the taut silence that followed.

Seconds later, he was amazed to see Colonel Pereira being led out of the jungle. He could hear the rebels spreading out in the bush, checking the vicinity for other intruders. He expected to hear more shots, see some evidence of the men who must have accompanied Pereira. Surprisingly, there was none.

Ross watched a furious Vargas questioning his captive at the edge of the clearing. They were too far away for him to hear anything. When he took a step in that direction, the guard threatened him again with the rifle. He stayed where he was, wondering if he looked as scared and worried as Anne and Dane.

The questioning was a lengthy one. Finally, Pereira was marched across the clearing and thrust roughly into the shelter with them. Three new sentries joined the young guard, ringing the structure on all sides. Vargas and several of his men had gone into one of the huts, presumably to confer. Elena accompanied them.

Ross wasn't challenged this time when he went to Pereira's side. "You hurt?"

The officer shook his head. "The shot missed me, and after that I had the good sense not to resist."

A shaken Dane, now on his feet, demanded, "Who is this guy, anyway? And what's he doing here?"

"I'd like an answer to that one myself," Ross drawled.

The colonel shrugged. "You couldn't expect me to just sit and wait, *Capitão*, until you and the *senhora* returned to the river. Your describing of the camp's location would have been useless by then. Once the rebels had the gold, they would have moved on and I would have lost them again."

"Yeah," Ross agreed dryly, "I should have known it was too easy when you sailed off."

"You turned around and followed us," Anne realized. "Why didn't we know?"

"Because I was never that close," he explained. "It wasn't necessary. We found someone in the village where your deck hand spent the night. He was willing to tell us of the inlet where the *Lady Odyssey* had gone. After that, it was simply a matter of tracking your trail. There are always signs for those who know how to see them. Remember, I have the Indian blood in me."

"Where are your men?" Ross wanted to know.

"Back at the gunboat, of course."

Anne was shocked. "You came here on your own?"

Pereira smiled at her wryly. "At the time, it seemed a wise decision. There were not enough of us to have conducted a successful raid and, alone, I could move more swiftly and silently."

"Evidently, not silently enough," Ross pointed out. "You were caught."

The colonel nodded. "And that was the *un*wise decision. I couldn't resist circling the camp to check on numbers and weapons. I was—forgive the indelicacy, *senhora*—discovered by a sentry who had stepped into the jungle to relieve himself. Had I instead returned at once to the inlet with the camp's location, the added forces we sent for would have been waiting for me to lead them to the rebels. The intention was to risk none of you. You would have either been on your way back by then, and well away from this place, or needing our assistance."

"Instead of which," Dane blamed him angrily, "you've gone and put us in danger."

"Shut up, Matthews," Ross told him impatiently. "Accusations aren't going to help."

Pereira sighed. "I am afraid he is right, *Capitão*. This Vargas suspects that you deliberately led me here. Now we are all of us at his mercy."

"But your people back at the gunboat...?" Anne said.

"Will not be able to find us without my directions. I am sorry, my friends."

There was nothing to say after that. The four of them, huddled in nervous silence, waited to learn Vargas's intention for them. They watched the entrance to the hut, but neither the rebel leader nor any of those with him emerged as the afternoon lengthened.

The sun was sliding behind the trees when Elena appeared. There was nothing friendly about her this time when she came to them in the shelter.

She reported the rebels' decision in a cold voice. "Vargas is an honorable man. He was ready to keep his promise because he trusted you. Now he feels he has been betrayed. You are all our hostages. We will leave here to find a new camp as soon as it is safe to move through the jungle, which will be at first light in the morning. The four of you will go with us and when the distance is sufficient, you will be released. Providing, of course, that you have not lied again and we are not being followed. Consider yourselves fortunate."

Pereira started to say something and Elena silenced him. "There is to be no argument and no questions. A meal will be brought to you now." She turned away and left them.

Minutes later, rice and beans, along with a suspicious-looking concoction that Dane identified as boiled bananas, was served to them in gourds. He informed him that these, as well as cassava beer, was a regular fare in the camp. They ate the mess with little appetite.

There was no opportunity for conversation. Immediately after supper and over Ross's objections, they were separated. The men were herded into a large hut where they were to spend the night under guard. Anne was left alone in the shelter.

Anne didn't expect to sleep, not when she was so frightened and worried and with the leg still throbbing angrily. But exhaustion overcame her, and in the end she drifted off on the cot.

It was late, the jungle wrapped in darkness, when she abruptly awakened, her heart racing in alarm. Earlier, much to her surprise, the rebels had placed a bamboo framework over the cot with netting draped around it to protect her from the nighttime infestation of mosquitoes. Now that netting was stirring as a hand furtively lifted it aside. She was no longer alone.

A deep whisper came out of the shadows. "Anne."

She sighed in relief at the sound of the familiar voice, then struggled to sit up. "Ross, what are you doing here? How did you get away?"

"Waited until our guard dozed off," he explained, ducking under the netting to join her. "Then I slipped out."

"Weren't there other guards?"

"Not inside the hut, but they've posted plenty all around the edges of the clearing. I don't think they're so worried about us as by what might sneak up on them out of the jungle. That's why the rest of them are collected around the campfire down at the far end there. They're edgy, afraid to go to sleep. They can't be sure Pereira's men wouldn't try to march on them, even though it's suicide to move through the jungle at night."

"I suppose that's why they didn't bother to leave any sentry with me. They knew I wasn't going anywhere, not with this leg."

He leaned over the cot. "It's worse instead of better, isn't it?"

"I—I don't know. It's still inflamed," she admitted, "and I wasn't able to stand on it very well when they brought the mosquito netting or when Elena helped me to use their bathroom facilities. Which, by the way, take the prize for crudeness."

Ross didn't answer her. She could feel how worried he was about her leg. She was concerned, too, and not just for herself.

"Ross, if they catch you out here, they could shoot you."

"Yeah, I know. That's why we have to be quiet."

"But if they should spot you moving around—"

"They won't. Look, I know that cot's pretty narrow, but do you think you could squeeze over far enough to let me slip in there with you? That way I won't be noticeable."

She wanted to refuse him, to insist that he go back to the hut where he would be safe. But she didn't because nothing was so bad when he was close to her. She needed him tonight and maybe he knew that. Silently, she shifted on the cot, making space for him.

Careful to avoid contact with her leg, Ross stretched himself beside her, gathering her into his arms. There wasn't anything sexual about their intimacy. In this situation, there couldn't be. But there was everything endearing and comforting in it. He held her against his warm, solid strength and she wasn't frightened anymore. She could face anything as long as he was with her.

They talked in low tones.

"You okay?" he asked.

"Yes." She paused. "Ross, why did you risk coming out to me? It wasn't just to check on my leg, was it?"

She wanted him to tell her he loved her and that he had to let her know this because tomorrow was so uncertain and if anything happened to them, there might not be another chance.

He didn't respond for a moment, and then when he did answer her, it wasn't anything she expected to hear. "Anne, we're so different. I don't mean just our life-styles. It's everything."

She heard sadness and regret in his voice. She turned her face toward him in surprise, trying to read his expression in the darkness. "How?" she whispered.

"The stuff that counts. Backgrounds mostly."

Why was he telling her this now, of all times? Why did he want her to know? It scared her. "You aren't saying anything you haven't already tried to say. Ross, I didn't want to listen then, and I don't now."

"Yes, you do, because there are things you don't know about me and should know. I was a hell-raiser growing up, Anne. Forever getting into trouble. All the bad junk. Running away, more than my share of brawling, too many of the wrong kind of friends. All right, so maybe a lot of that came out of loneliness and resentment—a mother who'd abandoned me, a father who didn't care enough to try relating to me—but it's still what I was."

"But you overcame all that. You went on to become an engineer and a caring husband and father."

She could feel him shaking his head. "A part of me is still that hell-raiser, Anne. And I think it was this wildness in me that helped foul up my marriage."

And would foul up any permanent relationship I tried. That's what he was essentially telling her. She had known he would ultimately try to convince her that he wasn't right for her, though she considered his timing to be lousy. She even understood why he felt this way. It was the result of too many emotional scars.

But it was maddening, his refusal to see his own worth, his inability to realize he was basically a decent and loving man. The man she wanted to belong to, the man she needed to share her life with.

"Ross," she whispered, "you're wrong. I know you're wrong. But I'm not going to argue with you. Not tonight. Tonight I just want you to hold me. That's all."

He did go on holding her while she managed to sleep again, secure in his arms. He hadn't been able to explain to her why he had joined her on the cot, why he had said what he had. It would have meant disclosing his intention to get her safely away from the rebels in the morning. And if he had shared that plan, she would have emphatically opposed it.

When she whimpered softly, still feeling the pain in her leg even in sleep, Ross knew he was right in his determination to see her returned directly to the inlet where the *Lady Odyssey* waited. He wanted her out of this mess and her leg professionally treated by doctors at a hospital. There was only one way he could think of to achieve this.

He waited until Anne was so deeply asleep that his leaving wouldn't rouse her again. Then, careful not to disturb her, he eased himself off the cot and left the shelter.

He didn't return to the hut. He walked toward the flickering fire where Vargas sat with his men.

Ross waited to tell the others until the four of them had been assembled in the open shelter at daybreak. They had been given fruit gathered from the wild and instructed that they were to eat this simple breakfast without delay. The rebels were anxious to move out.

"There's been a change in plan," Ross announced. Anne looked up from the stretcher they had rigged up for her, not liking the sound of his voice. Dane and Colonel Pereira, splitting papayas, paused to stare at him.

"I went to Vargas last night," Ross went on to explain in an unemotional voice. "I convinced him that they don't need four hostages to protect their getaway. They only need one. He was willing to buy that when I pointed out that with her leg, Anne would just be a handicap, slow them up. He's going to release her, permit her to go back to the inlet. Naturally, two of us will need to accompany her to carry the stretcher."

"Which two?" Dane demanded.

"You and Pereira."

"Which leaves you as the hostage," the colonel said. "Why the sacrifice, my friend?"

"I'm not being a hero," Ross insisted. "I'm just the logical choice. They would have preferred hanging on to you, of course, Colonel, until I suggested that a man of your age might be a liability on a long march through the jungle."

The officer smiled at him. "I don't know if I can ever forgive you that one, *Capitão*."

"Colonel, I need you back at that gunboat, using your authority to get Anne to a hospital quickly. Besides, you know how to find your way over the trail since they're unwilling now to send the Indian guide with you. Kona is needed to help them locate a new camp."

"No," Anne cried. "It's crazy! Elena promised that the four of us would be released as soon as the rebels get far enough away! But this way, you'd be all alone trying to make it back, and—"

"Anne," he interrupted her, "I'm the one who stands the best chance of making it back, especially if I can persuade them to give me a map and directions when they finally let me go. I know the jungle well enough to survive. Matthews doesn't. It's that simple."

Anne stared at him in a wild and angry frustration. She understood now why he had chosen last night to insist that they could never be right for each other. He had known when he joined her on the cot what he was going to arrange with Vargas. He realized there was a risk of his never getting out of the jungle alive. If that happened, if he didn't survive, then he didn't want her to live with regrets. He meant her to go away not wanting him. As if she could actually stop loving him just because he maintained they were too different to ever forge a lasting relationship. As if she would suffer less if anything happened to him and he didn't return.

There was something else she understood. His calculated argument last night had been the result of desperation. The kind of desperation that is evidence of a self-sacrificing love.

He loved her, and the realization should have filled her with joy. Instead, it only deepened her anger. Sitting up on the stretcher, she could feel her arms start to wrap around herself in the old, self-protective habit. No! She wasn't going to do that anymore! She found another way to handle her emotions. She railed at him furiously.

"You're a fool! If you can't think of anyone else, think of your missing son! What chance does Danny stand of ever being recovered if you never come back?"

Ross, ignoring her plea, crouched down at the side of her stretcher. He smiled at her out of the stubble of beard on his obstinate jaw. "There's something I never told you," he said to her so softly that the others couldn't hear. "You're a beautiful woman, Anne Richmond. Beautiful in that strong, special way that makes a man always remember. I wanted you to know that."

It was his form of goodbye. Casual and easy and absolutely heartbreaking.

Elena appeared in the shelter and touched him on the shoulder. "It's time," she said.

Ross nodded and got to his feet. He turned to Colonel Pereira with a message for Luiz. "Tell Luiz to move the *Lady Odyssey* to his cousins' village and wait for me there."

Anne, realizing that the moment of separation had arrived and that there was nothing she could do to prevent it, felt the helpless tears well in her eyes. "Ross, please," she begged him.

He refused to answer her. But she knew what was in his mind—*Let me do this for you, Anne. I couldn't do it for Claire, and I couldn't do it for Danny. But I can do it for you. Let me make you safe.*

"Take her out of here now, Pereira," Ross instructed the officer, "before Vargas changes his mind."

The colonel and Dane lifted the stretcher and started for the opening to the trail. Anne couldn't bear to look back.

She didn't want her last image of Ross to be blurred by a haze of tears.

The forest swallowed them. Minutes later, Dane's voice penetrated her misery. "What was that all about there at the end? You said something to him about his missing son?"

Dane was at the back of her stretcher. Anne twisted her head around to look up at him in surprise. There had been a curious interest in his tone. That same interest was on his face.

Nine

Ross stumbled out of the jungle two days later, looking like a desperado. He was unshaven, filthy, his clothes nearly in rags, and he was grateful to be alive. There had been moments in that sweltering hellhole after the rebels had released him when he never expected to see the sun again. But there it was, burning down on the river, and it was a welcome sight.

Ross sank down on the riverbank in exhaustion, savoring the open situation that allowed him to feel moving air on his face. Nothing had seemed to stir in the jungle, except the snakes and the vicious insects.

Knowing his rivers as well as he did, he was fairly certain that this was the Jara, but he had no idea where he had emerged along its length. He wasn't sure whether he should walk upstream or downstream to reach the settlement where, hopefully, the *Lady Odyssey* was waiting.

He had a slice of luck. He was still resting on the riverbank when a mestizo, fishing from his dugout, glided into view. Ross got to his feet, hailing the dugout. When he was finally able to convince its occupant that he was no *bandido*, the man took him aboard. The mestizo knew of the village Ross wanted. It was only a few miles upstream and, yes, he would take him there.

Less than an hour later, rounding a bend, Ross happily sighted the *Lady Odyssey* moored at the dock below the settlement. Equally pleasing to him was the figure of Luiz leaning over the bow rail. The scarred, skinny deck hand, recognizing him in the dugout, shouted and waved.

Minutes later, Ross was collapsed at the dinette table aboard the yacht with Luiz in the galley scrambling a pan of eggs for him. He couldn't remember when he had last eaten anything, and he was suddenly limp with hunger. He wanted to know everything that had happened in his absence, but first he had to eat.

It wasn't his deck hand, however, who ended up telling him what he longed to hear. He was devouring a plate of eggs Luiz slapped in front of him when Dane Matthews appeared. Ross was surprised. He hadn't expected to find the photojournalist here.

"You made it back." Dane greeted him with a slow, enigmatic smile. "Somehow I knew you would."

Ross stopped eating to stare at him. "Anne." He needed to know. "Is she all right?" He'd realized she must have reached the inlet with Pereira and Matthews, or Luiz wouldn't have known to move the boat to the village. But he wanted to be sure that she was safe.

Dane joined him at the table. "She's fine. There's a government landing strip a few miles upriver. When we got to the inlet, Colonel Pereira radioed from the gunboat. They sent a plane to fly her to Manaus. Since then, Pereira has been up and down the river in the gunboat looking for signs of you and the rebels. He stopped back here with the radio report that Anne is in a hospital and recovering from the infection.''

Ross experienced conflicting emotions—relief that Anne was free of danger and regret that she was out of reach. ''You didn't go with her,'' he said. ''Why?''

Dane shook his head. ''No, I didn't go with her. She fought against leaving. She wouldn't let them put her on the plane until I promised to stay here until you were safe.''

''And you agreed,'' Ross said, beginning to sense that there was a reason for Dane's generosity.

''I didn't mind. I spent the time developing my photographs. The plane was able to bring me the necessary equipment.''

''That was going to quite a bit of trouble, wasn't it? You could have waited until you got down to Manaus.''

''I had a reason.''

Dane's smile had deepened. Ross suddenly no longer had an appetite. He put down his fork. ''Something tells me I'm about to hear it.''

''I think you'll be interested,'' Dane said confidently.

Ross realized that he didn't like this man very much, and it had nothing to do with his being Anne's ex-husband. It was because, as Anne had once admitted, Dane Matthews was a manipulator, quick to take advantage of a situation. Ross sensed that he was about to try that very thing now. ''Go on,'' he said tautly.

''I have one of those photographs to show you,'' Dane explained, tapping the breast pocket of his shirt. ''Let me tell you, though, how I came to get this particular shot. You remember back at the camp when I told you that my Indian guide had us all over the map before we reached the rebels?''

Ross nodded.

''Well, we came through another small camp on the way. It belonged to this eccentric old guy living a hermit's existence right there in the forest. From his accent, I figured he must have been originally European. Not a native, anyway. He wasn't happy about seeing us there, didn't even want to give us a night's shelter until I paid him more than it was worth. The Indian thought that was because the guy existed by trading illegal pelts from the jaguars and otters he hunted and he was reluctant to let us discover this."

"Matthews, what has this to do with—"

"Wait," Dane interrupted him, holding up his hand. "It gets better. You see, this guy wasn't altogether alone. No, he had someone else living there with him. A kid. A boy. Maybe five, six years old."

Ross's mouth went dry and he stared at Dane with eyes that burned.

"Yeah, I thought you might like this part. That's where the photograph comes in. The kid was cute. I took a picture of him. The old guy went wild over that, almost smashed my camera. Said the boy had been a gift to him from the monkeys, but that the monkeys were jealous and would take him back if they knew where he was, so he kept him a secret. Crazy old bird, but I promised I wouldn't tell. Hell, I just figured the kid was his. I forgot all about it. That is, until on the way to the inlet I got Anne to tell me about your missing son. You see, I remembered that the kid had green eyes. About the color of yours, McIntyre."

Ross found that the hand he extended across the table was shaking. "The picture," he demanded, and his voice was trembling as well.

Dane produced the photograph and passed it to him. Ross gazed at the image of the small boy posed in the doorway of a rude hut. It was Danny. An older Danny, a changed Danny, but it was his son.

Emotion overwhelmed him, and it was a moment before he could find his voice again, asking hoarsely, "Was—was he all right?"

Dane shrugged. "He seemed pretty healthy to me. Happy enough, anyway. I guess he doesn't remember any other life. Nuts as the old guy is, he does care about the kid."

"Anne—"

Dane shook his head. "I didn't tell her why I was interested in your story. I figured this was between you and me."

Ross didn't care for the tone of his voice. "Where is this place?" he asked him tensely. "Could you find it again without the Indian guide?"

Dane nodded slowly. "I might remember the general location," he said carelessly. "I might even do better than that and remember where the Indian guide hangs out."

Ross, knowing he was right not to like Dane Matthews, understood him. There was a price for his knowledge. "All right, Matthews, suppose you tell me just what you want."

Dane didn't hesitate. "You agree not to see Anne again."

Ross's eyes narrowed warningly. "I'm not making any deals over Anne." He started to rise furiously from his chair. "But you're going to tell me what I want to know, Matthews, or I'll break your—"

"Easy, easy," Dane tried to soothe him, shaken by the menace in Ross's gaze. "All right, so that was a rotten thing for me to try, but I still want her."

Ross sank back in the chair. He suddenly felt almost sorry for the man. "You poor fool. You think this is the way to get her back?"

"I think I'd stand the chance if you weren't there confusing her emotions."

"I told you, no deals."

"Agreed. But before I tell you what you want to know, will you listen to me for a minute? Just do that much."

"Make it fast, because I've waited two years for this information and I'm clean out of patience."

Dane leaned toward him, pleading. "This isn't a matter now of you choosing your son over Anne. And it isn't a question of me, either. It's just you and Anne I want you to consider."

"What about us? Not that it's any of your business."

"You don't belong together," Dane told him bluntly.

"You're sure of that, huh?"

"I think so, and I think you know it, too. You're worlds apart, McIntyre. She ever tell you about her life in New Orleans aside from her work?"

"It didn't come up."

"Well, it's important to her. Things like the fund-raising dinner for the Friends of the Cabildo, the Spring Fiesta Ball, Mardi Gras parties in the Garden District, sitting on the board of Tulane. She's all of that, McIntyre. Can you honestly see yourself in that picture? Or maybe you figured on asking her to give that up and staying down here in Brazil. Maybe you'd want her to live on this old tub with you. She would probably do it, too, but in the end—"

"All right," Ross growled savagely, "you've made your point."

Dane wasn't telling him anything that he hadn't already told himself, but hearing it in specific detail made him realize more than ever that the kindest, most loving thing he could do for Anne was to let her go. It wasn't just a matter of conflicting life-styles. The truth was, he was scared by the depth of his feelings for her, afraid of ultimately failing her. Claire had been a painful lesson he was unable to forget. Okay, so that made him a coward, but he could live with that. He couldn't live with the risk of irreparably hurting Anne if their futures failed to mesh, if she began to see how impossibly different they were, or whatever her arguments now, if she started to regret their togetherness. But if he got out of her life now...

And there was his son to consider. He couldn't be sure how traumatic Danny's situation was or just how involved the recovery from his experience would be. But something told Ross that he would need to be there completely for Danny, maybe for a long time to come. And how fair would that be to Anne?

Ross's hands, down at his sides, curled into tight fists of helplessness as the sharp anguish of loss bit into his soul. He already missed her. He would probably miss her for the rest of his life, but that was a hell he could learn to survive. He had no other choice.

He felt Dane watching him, and he knew that the photojournalist understood his decision. He also knew what Ross wanted to tell him. *Don't celebrate. You don't have her just because I have to let her go, and I don't think you ever will. We've both lost her, Matthews.* But he didn't tell Dane that, because he knew the man wouldn't believe him.

Ross was aware that Luiz, hanging in the doorway, was also watching him. The deck hand couldn't have understood his conversation with Dane, but the sadness in his dark eyes told him that Luiz sensed his joy in finding Danny had been sapped by a painful surrender.

Ross heaved himself wearily to his feet, his fists planted on the edge of the table as he leaned toward Dane. "I'm going below to clean up. I want you to write down the directions to this place, anything and everything you can remember. I'll expect you to have it for me when I get back."

Ross headed for his cabin to shave and shower. He knew he ought to be crawling into his bunk, but he was prepared to ignore the rest his body was demanding. He wanted to get underway immediately. He wanted to reach Danny.

A half hour later, wearing fresh clothes, he returned to the dinette to find Colonel Pereira leaning over a map of the area spread on the table. Dane's directions were in his hand. Ross was surprised. He must have been under the shower when the gunboat arrived.

The officer looked up when he joined them, concern in his eyes as he discovered Ross's fatigue. "Welcome back, my friend."

"You don't sound thrilled about it, Colonel."

"Your return pleases me," Pereira said. "This intention of yours that Senhor Matthews has just shared with me does not."

Ross frowned. "Now look, Colonel, there's no way you're going to stop me from—"

Pereira held up a placating hand. "I am not suggesting for a moment that your son shouldn't be recovered as quickly as possible. What I am asking is that you permit me to do it for you."

"That's out of the question."

"Listen to me, please," the colonel appealed to him. "What I ask makes sense."

"How do you figure that?" Ross demanded.

"By looking at you. You are in no state to go back into the jungle again. How will it help the boy if you collapse on the way? Besides, this man who has him may be difficult to deal with, but I am official so he can't easily oppose that. It is the best way, *Capitão*."

"And what am I supposed to do in the meantime? Just sit here and go crazy?"

"I suggest you sail for Manaus. An army helicopter is being sent today from downriver. It was meant to scout for the rebels, but now we can use it to locate this man's camp. There is every chance for the helicopter delivering your son to you by the time the *Lady Odyssey* arrives in Manaus. It is better to get him straight out of the jungle. He may need the medical attention only Manaus can provide."

Ross longed to refuse him, to answer two long years of desperation by heading into the jungle without delay. But he recognized the wisdom of the colonel's argument. He didn't want to jeopardize Danny, to risk losing him again by charging wildly into the hermit's camp. The waiting would be terrible, but he would endure it for Danny's sake.

"All right," he agreed. "But I want constant radio contact. I want to know what's happening at all times."

"Agreed," Pereira said soberly.

Dane, who had been straddling a chair and listening silently, came slowly to his feet. "Colonel, you still expecting that plane with fresh supplies for the gunboat?"

"I am."

"Then maybe you wouldn't mind running me up to the landing strip with you. I'd like to see if I can beg a ride back to Manaus."

His intention didn't surprise Ross. He realized that Dane would want to get to Anne as quickly as he could.

Anne. Another torture waiting for Ross in Manaus. She would be there, and he would soon be there. The temptation of her nearness would somehow have to be resisted. He couldn't trust himself to see her. If he came anywhere close to her again, he might not be able to let her go. And he had to let her go. It would be the hardest thing he ever had to do and he didn't know how he was going to stand it, but he had to let her go.

Anne gazed at Dane from her elevated hospital bed, a naked longing in her voice as she asked, "Did Ross send any message for me?"

"No, nothing. I'm sorry."

"Oh, well," she said quickly, "it's understandable. He must have his mind full right now with his son's rescue. At least I know he's safe, and it's wonderful news about Danny." She didn't want Dane to see the depth of her disappointment, so she looked away, gazing at the exotic bouquet on her bedside table. "The flowers are beautiful. Thank you for bringing them."

He reached for her hand, holding it warmly in his. She hardly noticed in her distraction over Ross. "You'll be getting out of here soon, won't you?"

"Yes, I'm all right now, but the doctor refuses to release me. He says another two or three days. Apparently, it was a venomous spider and though I could have had a worse reaction, they want to make absolutely sure there's no nerve damage."

"When you do leave, what then?"

"That depends." On Ross, she thought, but she didn't tell Dane that.

"Anne?"

"Yes?"

"While you're waiting for that release, will you do something for me?"

"What is it?"

"Will you explore the possibility of our . . . well, getting back together again?"

Anne, finally understanding what this visit was really all about, stared at his blond good looks and was astonished. "Dane, you didn't think because I came to Brazil that I— What *did* you think?"

"I think you care. I think that under this infatuation for McIntyre, I still count. *We* count. Anne, you bought my release. You risked yourself to free me. That proves something, doesn't it?"

He was still holding her hand, persuasively stroking it. She snatched it away. "Dane, you've mistaken consideration for—for I don't know what. Not love, certainly. That's gone. It's over for us. It was finished years ago, and you're going to have to accept that."

"Anne, all this mess with the rebels happened because I wanted to prove to you that I could amount to something, and now you—"

"No!" She had to make him understand. She had to make him realize, even if it meant being brutally honest, that he was never going to manipulate her again with guilt. "What I did for you was purely out of conscience. You needed help and I couldn't ignore that. It would have been the same for anyone who had once been close to me. Nothing more."

"I can't believe—"

"Dane," she told him with a grave finality, "you have your life back. I don't owe you anything anymore."

She was sorry to hurt him, but he left her no choice.

His last words to her as he left her bedside were a solemn, "The guy isn't for you, Annie. He'll break your heart."

She thought about Dane's parting words through the rest of that long day and during most of the restless night that followed. She didn't believe for a moment what he had said to her, attributing his assertion to resentment. But he had left her worrying about a lot of unanswered questions. Where was Ross? When would he come to her? Was there something Dane had neglected to tell her?

By early afternoon the next day, Anne could no longer endure her inactivity. If she had to wait and try somehow to be patient about it, then she preferred to do so in the spacious comfort of a hotel. She phoned Gabriel Mendes at the Manaus branch of Richmond Pharmaceuticals and asked the Brazilian to fetch her.

The plump little nurse, who found Anne getting into her clothes five minutes later, protested her action. "Senhora Richmond, the doctor hasn't discharged you."

"I'm discharging myself," Anne told her firmly. "There's nothing wrong with me now and I'm sick of lying here. Don't worry. I'll check back with the doctor later, I promise."

Mendes was waiting for her in his car when she emerged from the hospital. The dapper little man had news for her as she joined him. "You said on the telephone that you were waiting for the arrival of Senhor McIntyre. But he is in Manaus already."

"Ross is here? Are you sure?"

"Of course. One of my people lives on a boat at the river. He told me after your call that the *Lady Odyssey* appeared this morning. The deck hand, Luiz, confided to him that McIntyre's son is being flown to him here."

Ross was in the city! Why hadn't he come straight to the hospital to see her? Why hadn't Dane told her that the *Lady Odyssey* was bringing him directly to Manaus, that he wasn't going after Danny himself? Maybe, Dane wouldn't want her to know that Ross was close by, but Ross might have contacted her. Something was wrong.

Mendes was waiting for her directions. "Will you stay again at the Hotel Fonte?"

"No. Yes. But take me to the waterfront first, please."

Anne tried to curb her anxiety as they wove through the heavy traffic. Within minutes, they were at the river and searching for the *Lady Odyssey*. Anne spotted the yacht first and pointed it out to Mendes. He was able to park within sight of the boat.

She started to slide eagerly from the car when the Brazilian touched her arm, drawing her attention to a military vehicle that was just pulling up close to the dock. At the same moment, Anne spotted Ross's tall figure striding forward to meet the new arrivals. The sight immediately aroused a familiar yearning. All her strained senses reached out to him.

He didn't see her. His attention was completely focused on the figures emerging from the military vehicle. Colonel Pereira appeared, his hand on the shoulder of a small, wide-eyed boy with shaggy dark hair and patched jeans that were far too big for him. Even at this distance Anne could see that he resembled Ross and how Dane had come to realize this. It was there in the boy's coloring and angular features, even in the way he held himself.

Anne watched, witnessing what she had never expected to be present for—the reunion of father and son. It was a moving scene when the colonel brought Danny forward, especially emotional considering all the harsh years and events that contributed to the realizing of it. Ross knelt in front of the boy, his face gentle and patient as Danny understandably viewed him with shyness and uncertainty. She could see how much Ross wanted to embrace his son and the effort his restraint was costing him.

Anne, her eyes misting, looked away. It suddenly occurred to her that this was a very private moment for them and that she had no right to intrude on it.

"Will you go to them?" Mendes asked her softly.

She shook her head, swallowing the thickness in her throat. "Not now. I think they need to be alone together. Take me to the hotel, Gabriel. I'll wait there."

The Brazilian was a good friend, she realized. He was concerned about her. After delivering her to the hotel and seeing her settled in a room, he promised to return early the next morning to take her back to the *Lady Odyssey*.

Anne found that waiting at the hotel was no better than the long, fretful hours she had spent in the hospital. In some respects, it was even lonelier. Her only companion was a softly humming air conditioner.

She spent her time thinking about Ross, wondering how he and his son were relating to each other. With joy, she hoped. She wanted to be with them. She wanted to be with Ross. Tomorrow, she promised herself.

She was picking at a breakfast tray she didn't really want when Gabriel Mendes rapped at her door the next morning. She hurried to let him in. When she saw his face, she knew at once that her uneasy feelings of yesterday had been justified.

"Tell me," she demanded, making an effort to keep her voice steady.

He shook his head sadly. "The man in our office I told you about, the one who lives on the river...he reports that Luiz is alone now on the boat. I went myself to check. I talked to Luiz. It is true. McIntyre turned the boat over to him."

"Where is Ross then?"

Mendes slowly, reluctantly told her the story. "He and his son have left the country. They flew back to North America late yesterday. Colonel Pereira expedited the matter. It was thought wise to get the boy quickly away from Brazil. The man who had kept him in the jungle opposed his being taken away and threatened to get him back. He had no right to him, naturally, but when he found him on the riverbank in a state of shock—where one presumes the child must have wandered after the death of his mother—and then took him in his dugout back to his camp..." The Brazilian shrugged. "Well, a regrettable situation for everyone, but then the man is not in his right mind or he wouldn't have kept the boy like that all this time."

Anne listened to Mendes's explanation and felt herself dying inside. She could sympathize with the old hermit's loss, understand his pain. Nothing was so cruel as a sharp, final separation from someone you had learned to love.

Ross was gone. He had left her. But not here in Manaus. In thinking back, she realized that he had really left her that morning in the rebel camp. His parting there had worn the quality of finality. She had refused to see it at the time, but somewhere deep inside herself she had known.

She knew Ross genuinely believed he was doing the right thing for her. She wondered if he would ever understand just how wrong he was, that instead of saving her from some eventual hurt by his foolish, self-sacrificing denial, he was condemning her to a life without the only man she would ever want.

Anne was suddenly angry with him. Angry that he had left without trying to see her, without so much as a message. Damn him, he hadn't the right to do this!

"But he had to do what he had to do." Her voice was brittle with irony, and she could feel a small, hysterical laugh threatening to erupt.

Gabriel Mendes, who must have been expecting tears, looked at her with worry in his dark eyes. "I beg your pardon?"

She shook her head. "Nothing. A line out of an old movie. Or close enough, anyway."

He went on watching her, his concern evident. "What will you do now, *senhora*?"

She turned away, gazing through the window at the sprawling city. "Go home. It's all I *can* do."

Anne fulfilled her decision later that same day as she boarded a flight heading for New Orleans. As the plane rose through a light scattering of stratus clouds, she looked through the window and saw the ocean of jungle spread below, veined by countless waterways. She thought of what had happened to her down there. A romantic adventure. That's what most people would call it. Except, she told herself, aching inside, you were supposed to survive the effects of romantic adventures. Maybe, given enough time, she would recover from hers. But she wasn't counting on it.

Ten

Ross was nervous with anticipation. The palms of his hands gripping the wheel of the rental car were actually sweating. Like a kid on his first big date, he thought with a wry smile. He drove slowly along the avenue framed in majestic live oaks, scanning the house numbers as he searched for the address Gabriel Mendes had given him during his call yesterday to Brazil.

A horn blared impatiently behind him, making him realize that in his anxiousness, he was all over the road. Damn! At this rate, he was going to end up in a wreck. He squeezed over to the side of the avenue and the convertible shot past him. At that moment, he sighted the number he was looking for.

Swinging into the driveway, he crawled past banks of well-tended azaleas, bringing the rental car to a stop in a parking area fronting the house. He shut off the engine, but he didn't get out. He sat there gazing at the house. It was long

and low, a contemporary-style dwelling overlooking Lake
Pontchartrain. It was a handsome home, but not nearly as
imposing as Ross had feared. Not the elegant traditional
mansion he had associated with Anne. Wisteria wreathed
the front door and the brick steps supported a variety of
potted plants. They made the place informal and friendly.

He didn't know if this house was going to welcome him,
though. The door might be slammed in his face. He
wouldn't blame her if that was his reception. He deserved
her anger.

Oh, hell, maybe this was a major mistake. He had no
right showing up here, turning her existence upside down
again after all these weeks. She was probably over him by
now, her life back on course, and he was about to make a
fool of himself. He couldn't help it. He had tried to resist,
but in the end, he could no longer fight it. He needed to see
her, be with her.

And there was something he *had* to let her know.

Squaring his shoulders, Ross climbed from the car. The
New Orleans air was balmy and serene, scented with blos-
som. It made him think that he should have brought flowers
for her, like the kid on his big date. There was a lot he
should have done before turning up here unexpectedly. For
instance, he ought to have written or phoned first. Instead,
he had impulsively jumped on that plane, too much of a
coward to chance an ignored letter or a call that wasn't returned. She was in his blood, all right. The long, agonizing
struggle he had finally lost with himself had convinced him
of that.

He mounted the steps and rang the bell. While he stood
there waiting for the door to be answered, he brushed at
imaginary lint on his gray pinstriped suit. He suddenly felt
uncomfortable and ridiculous in the suit. Why had he worn
it? It wasn't him. Another mistake.

The door was swung open so abruptly seconds later that Ross was startled. He found himself confronting a woman whose intimidating bulk filled the opening.

"Help you?" she asked.

On the surface, her greeting was pleasant enough, but he had the distinct impression that she was already suspicious of him. "Good morning. I'm here to see A—Ms. Richmond, that is."

The woman was in no hurry to accommodate him. Her shrewd gaze swept him from head to toe. Ross made an effort not to squirm under her scrutiny. He was certain of it now. The damn suit was all wrong. He would have been better off in his old jeans and a sweatshirt.

"And if she was at home, who would I say wanted her?"

"McIntyre. Ross McIntyre." He had dealt with tough individuals before, but this woman would have been a match for any mean gorilla he had ever encountered in a waterfront bar. What was her problem, anyway?

"Ross McIntyre, huh?" The name was familiar to her, he realized. What's more, she didn't care for it. She snorted in belligerence.

All at once Ross understood. He remembered Anne telling him about her best friend and housekeeper, Carrie. This, undoubtedly, was Carrie. Anne must have confided in her, told her everything. And Carrie resented him, convinced he had deeply hurt Anne.

"Ms. Richmond," Ross reminded her.

She frowned at him severely. "She's not here."

"Where can I find her, then?"

"She doesn't want to see you."

"Isn't that for her to say?"

Carrie didn't answer him. She went on standing there, arms akimbo, looking as stubbornly protective as a eunuch in a harem. There was no way around it. He would have to launch an appeal.

"Look," he said gently, "it's important. I think she'd want to hear what I've come to say. And if she doesn't— well, then I promise you I'll go away without bothering her. Please."

Carrie went on regarding him. He watched her displeasure soften to uncertainty and then finally to a reluctant surrender. "It's like I said. She isn't here. She's at work."

He hadn't been prepared for this possibility. It was Saturday morning and he had expected to find her at home. "Can I go to her there?"

Carrie nodded slowly. "I suppose you might. She's got herself all fixed to fly out to Dallas this afternoon on some business. Took her bag with her, so she's not coming back here. But it's still early. You shouldn't have trouble catching up with her at the office." She supplied him with directions to the corporate headquarters of Richmond Pharmaceuticals.

Ross grinned his gratitude. "Thank you, Carrie."

"You just remember that promise of yours." She shook her head. "Lord, I hope I'm doing the right thing here. She never said you were a big, sexy devil who could charm a woman into sin, but I just knew you had to be. And you are sure enough."

Ross didn't feel like any "sexy devil" as he drove swiftly away from the house. More than ever, he was that eager kid heading for his important date, his excitement mounting. And his palms were still sweating on the wheel.

Anne was at her desk in the sleekly appointed executive suite of Richmond Pharmaceuticals. For the past half hour, she had been studying the meticulously prepared presentation she was going to make to the owner of a chain of Texas pharmacies, hoping to convince him to carry Richmond products. Ordinarily, her sales manager would have been handling this assignment and she wouldn't have come into

her office on a Saturday, much less have scheduled herself
to fly out for the weekend to meet with a drugstore czar who
maintained unusual business hours. But since her return
from Brazil, she had kept herself as busy as possible in an
effort to numb her emotions. She wasn't successful. No
matter how full her calendar or how long her hours in the
office, unwanted images persisted in tugging at her senses.
Usually at the most inconvenient of times.

This was one of those moments. Her desk was posi-
tioned so that she had a generous view of the carefully
landscaped acres of the corporate park on the outskirts of
New Orleans. She had always considered the perspective
green and restful. This morning she found herself dis-
tracted by the grove of palmettos outside her window. They
reminded her of the lush growth of a tropical jungle.

Hopeless. She couldn't concentrate properly on the presentation. The words and figures kept blurring into a
meaningless morass. Everything seemed to lack meaning for
her these days—her work, her home, the social affairs she
forced herself to attend.

She laid the presentation on top of her briefcase along
with her reading glasses. Maybe she'd have better luck with
it on the plane.

She swung around in her chair so that the view was no
longer confronting her. It was no use. She should have been
looking at a paneled wall and a collection of tasteful prints.
Instead, she was seeing that same hot jungle, a long river
and a virile figure with an irreverent gleam in his compelling eyes. The disturbing memories wouldn't let her go.

She hadn't known it was possible to love so much. Nor to
hurt so deeply because of it. She had tried to make herself
believe that she could forget Ross, learn not to want him.
But her need hadn't softened any since she left Brazil. If
anything, it had sharpened. It made her more aware than
ever of the void of her life outside of her work. She had

Carrie, she had other friends, *good* friends, but she was lonely. She found herself wishing for the family she didn't have, the partner who would share her existence on all those levels essential to a woman, even a child, perhaps.

She had none of that. She'd had Dane after her mother and father had gone, but by then she hadn't wanted him. He had failed her. A friend, who had heard through the grapevine, recently told her that he was in New York now, trying to sell his rebel story and photos. She wished him luck, but she didn't care to see him again. She had no idea where Ross was at this moment, nor did she trust herself to try to find out. She was certain he didn't want to be located.

Anne leaned back restlessly in her chair. This was senseless, self-defeating. All right, she missed Ross. A part of her would always miss him, yearn for him, but she couldn't go on wallowing in hopeless daydreams. She owed it to herself and her company to get on with the business of living.

She was reaching again for the presentation when her assistant interrupted her, sweeping in from the outer office on a wave of jasmine scent. "Here's the final info you needed." The cheerful brunette placed a computer printout in front of her. "And the airline just called. They have a cancellation on this morning's Dallas flight, which you were originally hoping for. You could still make it if you leave now."

Perfect, Anne thought. She wouldn't have to hang around here indulging in nonproductive fantasies until she caught the afternoon flight.

"Sounds good," she agreed. "Gail, would you call me a cab while I gather my stuff? I think I'll leave my car garaged here in the underground. With the time so close, I don't want to have to deal with that traffic out to the airport. Oh, in case I didn't mention it, thanks for coming in this morning. I really appreciate it."

There was no traffic along the frontage road except for the taxi that flew past him, headed in the opposite direction, as Ross sought the entrance to the corporate park.

Seconds later, he was on the access lane, searching the scattered high-rise office buildings for Richmond Pharmaceuticals. He found it in the center of the expansive park—an impressive structure of steel and glass. He wouldn't permit himself to dwell on the realization that Anne was in charge of all this. He was already tense enough as he parked the rental car in the visitor's lot and started for the glass doors.

It was the weekend and the lobby was deserted except for a balding security man who looked up from his magazine, smiling at him politely. "Can I help you, sir?"

"I was told I could find Ms. Richmond here this morning."

The guard shook his head. "You just missed her. She left in a cab not ten minutes ago."

Ross's heart sank. "Going where?"

"Sorry, I can't help you with that. Here's someone who might, though. Gail is Ms. Richmond's assistant." An attractive brunette had emerged from one of the elevators and was crossing the lobby on her way to her car.

Ross stopped the woman and introduced himself, explaining his need to reach Anne. She considered him with interest, also a touch of misgiving. But his earnestness was convincing.

"There was a cancellation on an earlier flight," she confided, "so she decided not to wait until this afternoon. But if it's important, I suppose..."

"It is," Ross assured her. "Urgent, in fact." He wasn't exaggerating. He was feeling that urgency increase by the moment. He couldn't wait for her return from Dallas. He had to be with her now. It was all that mattered suddenly, and if he missed her...

Gail made up her mind. "Well, maybe you can still catch her at the airport. Southern Airways, flight 501. It's due to leave at—"

But Ross was already thanking her and on his way out of the building, racing for his car.

The drive to the airport couldn't have been more frustrating. The traffic was heavy and aggravatingly slow. Ross was unfamiliar with the route, so he took the wrong exit ramp from the expressway and had to backtrack. Conscious of the waste of precious minutes, of a delay that might easily cause him to lose her, he heard himself pleading eloquently. "Wait for me, Anne. I don't deserve it after Manaus, but wait for me."

By the time Ross arrived at the Southern Airways departure gate, the flight had been fully boarded, though the jetway had yet to be retracted. There was still time, if only this fool of a gate attendant would listen to him.

"Sir, I'm sorry, but I really can't let you on that plane. They'll be closing the doors any minute now, and since you're not a passenger..."

"Give me your pen," Ross commanded the man brusquely.

"What?"

"Your pen! Quick!" Thinking fast, he had decided what he had to do. If he tried to pressure this guy into letting him on board, it could be too late. The plane might leave while they argued about it.

He withdrew from his pocket the slip of paper on which he had written Anne's home address yesterday after calling Brazil. The bemused gate attendant handed him his ballpoint. Ross seized it and crossed out the address part, leaving only Anne's full name across the top. Then he turned the paper over and rapidly scrawled his simple message on the back.

In seconds he was thrusting the note at the gate attendant. "Please, it's an emergency. Just have a flight attendant hand her this. I promise I'll wait right here."

The young man hesitated, then accepted the note. Ross watched him turn and hurry along the jetway. Then he prayed.

"Ms. Richmond?"

Anne, settled in an aisle seat, looked up into the lively face of the stewardess bending toward her. "Yes?"

"This is for you. From a gentleman out in the gate area."

Mystified, Anne accepted the scrap of paper the woman extended toward her. It had been folded in half, her name appearing along one side. She opened it and turned it over. There were only two words on it in a bold and imploring hand: *Don't go!*

There was no signature, but Anne *knew*. Instinctively and instantly she knew, and hope broke through her long despair like a shining orb. She suddenly felt lighthearted, reckless.

Her fingers were fumbling at the buckle of her seat belt when apprehension gripped her. Wait a minute! What was she doing? She was rushing to him without pride when he had walked out on her without a word. Now, out of nowhere, he was back and expecting—what? She wouldn't know if she didn't go to him. She would never know if she let this plane carry her out of his life. And she would regret it for the rest of her days. This was no time for pride or caution.

Anne was up from her seat in a flash, reaching for her briefcase and small carryall, calling frantically to the stewardess, "Please, I have to get off the plane. It's very important."

The woman was understanding. She seemed to read it all in Anne's face. Without question or a word of opposition, she was helping her toward the exit with an encouraging, "There's just time. Have you got everything?"

Anne wasn't sure she did, nor did she much care. All that mattered was that she was off the plane now and moving back along the jetway. He was waiting for her as she emerged into the gate area, and her heart soared at the sight of him.

She couldn't believe her eyes. The remembered image of him she'd treasured had been dressed in that ridiculous skipper's cap and a pair of scruffy jeans while he stood potently at the helm of the *Lady Odyssey*. This was an unfamiliar Ross, though not a less breathtaking one, in a slim gray suit that emphasized his dark, rugged good looks.

The rush of relief Ross felt at her appearance was heightened by his rediscovery of her grace and elegance. God, she looked good! She was more alluring than he remembered in that tailored blue dress that suited her soft blond hair and showed her silken legs to advantage. Hell, he was actually wobbly in the knees!

They moved toward each other and then stopped a few paces apart, gazes betraying a nervous uncertainty for both of them. Anne was dimly aware of the whine of jet engines behind her, of her larger luggage flying off to Dallas without her. It wasn't important.

Ross's eyes, deep and somber, searched hers. "Yeah," he said, his voice low and gruff with emotion, "I'm out of uniform."

She smiled. "Me, too. I got used to the pants and shirt while we were on the river."

The sultry voice he had missed so much, along with her subtle fragrance, tantalized him. He wanted to sweep her up into his arms, hold her, never let her go. But he was afraid to touch her, afraid of her reaction.

"Ross?"

"I know. But not here, huh? What I have to say is...well, it needs real privacy. Is there somewhere we can go?"

Anne answered without a moment's consideration. "Richmond keeps a hospitality suite right here at the airport hotel. If you'd like..."

He didn't hesitate. "Let's go."

She didn't know just how they got to the hotel and up into the attractive suite overlooking the Mississippi. She was in such a daze that she was still finding it hard to believe he was actually here close beside her, warm and solid and real.

But once the door had closed behind them and they stood alone together in the silence of the spacious sitting room, she was suddenly aware of the adjoining bedroom with its massive four-poster bed visible through the open door. A sense of panic engulfed her. Why had she brought him here? They could have talked privately in any number of *safe* places—the airport coffee shop, a bench outside the terminal, even in his car. But this seclusion was so—so suggestive. Would he think she had misunderstood him? After all, she didn't know why he had come, what this thing was he had to tell her. It might have nothing whatever so do with what she was so desperate to hear.

"Let's sit down," she suggested, surprised at the control in her voice. She settled on a loveseat, indicating a matching sofa across from her.

Ross perched on it facing her, knees apart, suit coat unbuttoned. He hated this! He hated her sitting there all calm and polite with one shapely leg crossed over the other, the damn coffee table between them while the lure of her scent drove him crazy. He wanted to drag the table out of the way, haul her into his arms and cover her everywhere with his mouth. He couldn't. He had to quell his urge. He had some difficult explaining to do first, and afterward...well, he didn't know. The uncertainty scared him.

"How did you track me to the airport?" she asked.

He cleared his throat. "Oh, well, I went to your home and your friend Carrie sent me to your office. They told me there. I don't think Carrie approves of me."

Anne smiled. "Carrie is all mush under the armor."

"Yeah?"

Anne watched him, seeing how his big hands dangled between his knees, the way he sat awkwardly on the edge of the sofa. She had never seen him uncomfortable like this before, almost boyishly vulnerable, and it touched and amazed her. He was as nervous as she was!

She leaned forward, trying to help him. "How's Danny? Is he okay?"

She watched his face glow with pride at the mention of his son. "He's a wonderful kid, Anne. We're getting to know each other all over again. He doesn't remember much. He was so little when it happened and he went through so much, but he's going to be fine."

"Well, they're pretty resilient at his age, aren't they? Did he come to New Orleans with you?"

Ross shook his head. "He's waiting for me back in Florida. I left him with Claire's folks." He saw her surprise and he shrugged. "I know. I didn't approve of the way they raised their daughter, and I wasn't exactly their favorite son-in-law. But they lost Claire, and Danny is the only grandson they'll ever have. I figure they're entitled to share him."

Anne nodded slowly, thinking what she couldn't bring herself to say because there was still this awful wall stretched between them.

There's a reason why your Danny is "a wonderful kid." It's because he has such a wonderful father.

There was another clumsy silence, and she decided she could take the suspense no longer. "Ross," she said through the sudden constriction in her throat, "why are you here in New Orleans? What is this—this important thing you want me to know?"

He looked down briefly at his hands still between his knees, then lifted his gaze again to meet hers. She saw him swallow as he searched for the words, and she knew how difficult this was for him. For both of them.

"Leaving you like that in Manaus without a word," he said, "was a pretty rotten thing to do after—well, after what we'd had together. But I knew you knew why I was doing it. Why I *had* to do it."

"Yes, I knew. You thought you could never be for me what you felt I needed in my life, but—"

"No, listen. It was a confusing time for me, Anne. I just wasn't thinking straight with all that was happening. Then when I got back to Florida and there was time to sort it all out . . ."

"What?"

"Well, see, it hit me all at once. I remembered that night when we were alone on the boat and I tried not to want you. I told you it couldn't work, that being the kind of guy I was I'd only hurt you if we—"

"Made love."

"Yeah. And then you came to my cabin and you said I had no right to make your decision for you, that you were responsible for your own choices. That's what I remembered in Florida, Anne."

"That you'd gone and made another decision for me when you left Manaus," she said, understanding him.

"That's it. I was doing it again. I wasn't giving you the chance to choose for yourself. That's what it all boils down to." He bent toward her eagerly. "And that's why I'm here in New Orleans."

"To let me choose for myself."

He nodded quickly and she could see the worry in his eyes, hear the strain in his voice. "So if you still want . . . that is, if you still care— Well, maybe I am all wrong for you, maybe that hasn't changed, but— Look, I thought I could do it. I thought I could let you go. Damn it, I can't because I'm in love with you and I sensed you felt the same, and if it isn't too late . . ." There was nothing more he could say.

The silence that followed was the worst he had ever endured. She just sat there staring at him. He couldn't stand it. "No?" he whispered desolately.

She took a slow, deep breath. "Yes," she answered him simply. "Oh, yes."

It was the only incentive he needed, all he had been waiting for, praying for. He was on his feet and thrusting aside the barrier of the coffee table. Then he was on the sofa with her, doing what he had longed to do from the moment she had walked off that plane.

His arms went around her and he crushed her against him with a proprietary need that, if he had paused to consider it, would have awed him in its fierceness. But he was too busy to think, his hungry mouth branding every part of her face with his assertive kisses while his confessions, as broken and wild as his kisses, poured out of him.

"I was afraid of commitment. Afraid it would all go wrong for us."

She clung to him with a joyous, breathless laughter as his lips continued their rampage over her eyes, nose, cheeks. Between his kisses, he went on spilling his confessions.

"In the end, though, I was more afraid of going on alone. Sitting there in Florida, I realized I wasn't worth much without you."

"Yes."

"And it was awful, you know. Nothing was any good without you. Nothing was right."

"I do know. There wasn't a minute when I wasn't missing you, even when I was hating you for leaving me like that."

"Don't talk now, sweetheart," he commanded. "Don't talk anymore."

"Don't talk?" she said, still choking on laughter. "But you're the one who—"

"Shh," he hushed her, his hands framing her face now. "Let me concentrate."

She permitted him to do just that. His lips angled across hers in a slow, deep, lingering kiss. The fusion of their mouths, his tongue mating with hers, invoked a shuddering pleasure in her, a smoldering arousal in him. She could feel the hard ridge of his swollen flesh straining against her hip.

His mouth lifted from hers with a long sigh. He rested his forehead against her brow, and his voice was thick and rough with desire. "If I don't touch you soon, I'll go out of my mind."

"And exactly what," she wondered, "have you been doing for the last—"

"No." His forehead shook hers, and his shoulder dipped in the direction of the bedroom. "Not out here. In there."

"Understood," she complied happily as he drew her to her feet. Arm snug around her waist, he walked her toward the bedroom and the four-poster waiting for them.

Now it makes sense, Anne thought, smiling to herself. On some subliminal level, she must have known all along what she was doing bringing him up here to the suite. The airport coffee shop certainly wouldn't have suited this situation. Oh, Lord, she was delirious! They were both a little crazed with happiness.

It can't get any better than this, she thought.

But as she learned a moment later in the bedroom, happiness is always subject to improvement. With their clothes hastily shed and strewn everywhere on the floor, Ross folded her against his hard, naked length and proceeded to introduce her to the ultimate degree of euphoria.

His kisses were warm, wet, enticing, his seduction powerful as he slowly rubbed his hair-roughened chest back and forth across her breasts, abrading her nipples until she was convulsed with hot tremors. Then his lowered lips homed in on her sensitized breasts, drawing in turn each turgid nipple into the cavern of his mouth with a forceful, leisurely suction.

She withstood the prolonged onslaught of his caressing tongue. But when his hand pressed between her thighs and began to stroke, building a liquid fire, she writhed against him, her body pleading for a union with his.

Ross understood her silent beseeching. "All right, sweetheart," he rasped. "All right."

Supporting her with one hand, dragging aside the bedspread with the other, he tumbled with her across the bed. For a moment, they were all entwined limbs and a frenzy of misdirection generated by their long absence from each other. Ross, easing her frustration with his swift kisses, guided her finally into the position that would make their blending possible.

"We belong to each other now," he promised, his voice a fervent rumble as he entered her.

She knew it was true, and she reveled in their joining, in the stunning rhythms their clasped bodies achieved. With mindless cries and the perfect miracle of their oneness, they searched for and captured the volcanic pinnacle together.

Drowsy with completeness, they slept in each other's arms. Minutes later, Ross awakened to find that, incredibly, he was still hard inside her. His muscular body stirred, seeking a renewal of their satisfaction. Anne responded to his need with her own sinuous movements, and again they surged toward a consummate fulfillment.

Even through the long inertia that followed, his possessiveness was evident, demonstrated by his leg curled over hers, his arm tight around her waist as they lay side by side.

"Do you suppose," he wondered, "that we'll ever get enough of each other?"

She smiled happily. "I hope not."

She could feel his chin nodding against the top of her head. "Yeah, I don't think we will. We'll probably be at each other morning, noon and night. Assuming, that is..."

She caught the trace of worry in his voice, and she turned her face toward his. "What?"

"That we're sharing the same household."

"Won't we be?"

"Well, that's the plan. The only thing is, I'm kind of an old-fashioned guy once you get under all the raw layers. But if you don't feel you can put up with me as a husband—"

"Whoa! Is this a proposal?"

"I think it is. Only, like I say, if marriage is out of the question, then—"

"And who said anything about not accepting your proposal?"

He gazed at her with an endearing, eager glow in his eyes. "Yeah?"

"Yeah."

His eyes turned solemn then. "Anne, I promise you that I'll do my damnedest to fit into your world. I'll try never to be threatened by—"

She put a finger against his mouth, silencing him. "McIntyre, what do I have to do to convince you that I'm not a part of that scene? Want to know who my closest friend is after Carrie? A street artist who does tourist portraits over in Jackson Square. Then there's the elementary teacher I worked with before my father recruited me for Richmond. You'll like her and her husband. He has a small construction outfit, and they have a boy about Danny's age. Just ordinary, nice people."

"Not New Orleans high society, huh?" he asked, thinking of what Dane had tried to tell him.

She shook her head. "Only in connection with business or the charities I support, because I am proud of New Orleans. But it's not my regular life-style."

His nose nuzzled her cheek. "You're a pretty special woman, aren't you? A *giving* woman."

She chuckled softly. "Why? Just because I'm interested in preserving my city?"

"No, because you care about people. Luiz told me that he's scheduled to deliver a spinet piano you ordered for the chapel at Sister Veronica's mission school."

She was surprised by his knowledge. "You spoke to Luiz?"

"Among others. My phone bill to Brazil is going to set records. I had to arrange financing so that Luiz and a cousin of his could buy the *Lady Odyssey* from me. I can't afford to just turn the boat over to them. I need the funds to set myself up in business. What do you think? Can New Orleans use another independent engineer?"

Anne pressed a kiss on his shoulder. "When they hear how smart he is, he'll be up to his ears in work."

"I am smart," he growled softly at her ear. "Smart enough to fall in love with a woman who didn't give up on me through all my black moods, who made me feel that I could be a whole man again. And I was even smart enough in the end to realize that I'd better not lose her."

She clung to him, moved by his declaration. "Oh, Ross," she confessed with a small, shaky laugh, "she isn't so wonderful. Right now, she's suddenly worried and a little scared."

"What?" he demanded.

"Danny. I want so much for him to accept me, to accept that we're going to be a real family. Only I don't have any experience with mothering, none at all, and what if—"

"Hey, it's going to be easy. If you could tame his old man's angry heart, then Danny is going to be a pushover."

"You think so?"

"I know so. You can do anything."

"*We,*" she corrected him. "Together."

"Yeah, together. That's a good word, isn't it?"

"The best," she agreed with a smile of contentment. "Only the very best."

* * * * *

proudly presents
the long-awaited ''prequel'' volume of

LOVE AND GLORY

by
LINDSAY McKENNA

Dawn of Valor

In the summer of '89, Silhouette Special Edition premiered three
novels celebrating America's men and women in uniform: LOVE
AND GLORY, by bestselling author Lindsay McKenna. Featured
were the proud Trayherns, a military family as bold and patriotic
as the American flag—three siblings valiantly battling the threat
of dishonor, determined to triumph... in love and glory.

Now, discover the roots of the Trayhern brand of courage, as
parents Chase and Rachel relive their earliest heartstopping
experiences of survival and indomitable love, in

Dawn of Valor, Silhouette Special Edition #649.

This February, experience the thrill of LOVE AND GLORY—from
the very beginning!

DV-1

FEBRUARY FROLICS!

This February, we've got a special treat in store for you: four terrific books written by four brand-new authors! From sunny California to North Dakota's frozen plains, they'll whisk you away to a world of romance and adventure.

Look for

L.A. HEAT (IM #369) by Rebecca Daniels
AN OFFICER AND A GENTLEMAN (IM #370) by Rachel Lee
HUNTER'S WAY (IM #371) by Justine Davis
DANGEROUS BARGAIN (IM #372) by Kathryn Stewart

They're all part of February Frolics, coming to you from Silhouette Intimate Moments—where life is exciting and dreams do come true.

FF-1

Silhouette romances are now available in stores at these convenient times each month.

Silhouette Desire
Silhouette Romance

These two series will be in stores on the 4th of every month.

Silhouette Intimate Moments
Silhouette Special Edition

New titles for these series will be in stores on the 16th of every month.

We hope this new schedule is convenient for you. With only two trips each month to your local bookseller, you will always be sure not to miss any of your favorite authors!

Happy reading!

Please note there may be slight variations in on-sale dates in your area due to differences in shipping and handling.

WRITTEN IN THE STARS

**Star-crossed lovers?
Or a match made in heaven?**

Why are some heroes strong and silent...and others charming and cheerful? The answer is WRITTEN IN THE STARS!

Coming each month in 1991, Silhouette Romance presents you with a special love story written by one of your favorite authors—highlighting the hero's astrological sign! From January's sensible Capricorn to December's disarming Sagittarius, you'll meet a dozen dazzling and distinct heroes.

Twelve heavenly heroes...twelve wonderful Silhouette Romances destined to delight you. Look for one WRITTEN IN THE STARS title every month throughout 1991—only from Silhouette Romance.

STAR

COMING IN FEBRUARY FROM

SILHOUETTE® *Desire*™

Western Lovers

An exciting new series by Elizabeth Lowell
Three fabulous love stories
Three sexy, tough, tantalizing heroes

In February,   *Man of the Month* Tennessee Blackthorne in
                 OUTLAW
In March,   Cash McQueen in *GRANITE MAN*
In April,   Nevada Blackthorne in *WARRIOR*

WESTERN LOVERS—Men as tough and untamed as
the land they call home.

Only in *Silhouette Desire*!